THE PLEDGE

CHANDRA
SPARKS TAYLOR

THE PLEDGE

THE PLEDGE

ISBN-13: 978-0-373-83098-5
ISBN-10:   0-373-83098-X

www.KimaniTRU.com

Printed in U.S.A.

To my Jessie girl. May you always know how much your mommy loves you and above all else, love God and yourself. I hope I've made you proud.

Acknowledgments

I am so humbled to have the opportunity to once again pen my acknowledgments. God is so good, and just as He promised, in His due season, my life is unfolding just as it should. To Him goes all the glory and the honor.

To Jessica, who fuels me every day. I love you beyond words. Thank you for making so many of my dreams come true.

To my family: my parents, the late Cedric Sparks and the late Doris Sparks; my brothers, Andra and Cedric; my sisters-in-law, Karen and Pam; my nieces and nephews, Anthony, Brittany, CJ, DeJa and Chancellor; the Sparkses; the Joneses; my grandparents, George and Lela Jones and the late Ida B. Sparks; my great-aunt Rosie Mae O'Bryant; and Curtis and Jamaal Taylor. Thank you for all your love and support.

To my friends: Allilsa Bradley, Toni Staton Harris ('ppreciate it! LOL.), Nancey Flowers, the Richardsons, Calvin and Beverly Lawrence, Angela Coppins, Tamala Maddox, Adrienne Jeanine Durr, Kim Locke Crockett, my Bible-study buddies (Darlene, Beverly, Bonnie and Nancey) and my church families at 45th Street, First Baptist and Shiloh.

To Kris White and Darryl Oliver. Thank you for your help with the sports info.

To the real Courtland, whom I met during my signing at Colonial Brookwood. Thanks for letting me use your name.

To the schools, libraries and organizations across the country, but especially in Birmingham, Alabama—and especially Denise Allen at the West End Library—who have so graciously opened their doors to me. I can't wait to visit again soon.

To the staff of Kimani Press, especially Glenda Howard. Thank you for your belief in me and for entrusting me with Courtland Murphy's story.

Finally, to the readers. Thank you for your e-mails, reviews and enthusiasm for *Spin It Like That*. Growing up, I always dreamed about writing books that focused on African-American young adults because there weren't many stories about people who looked like me. Thank you for sharing my dream. i would love to come to your school or library to meet you in person. Have your school or library official contact me at cstwrites@aol.com or visit me at www.chandrasparkstaylor.com to arrange a visit. Until we meet, keep the e-mails coming. I love hearing from you. I pray you enjoy reading *The Pledge* as much as I enjoyed writing it. God bless you, and may your wildest dreams come true.

one

Adrenaline fueled me, and I sucked in a calming breath before running at full speed toward the Astroturf, clapping and grooving to the beat as I got into formation for our homecoming halftime show.

I quickly scanned the crowd, searching for my own personal cheering squad—my mother, my little sister, Cory Murphy, my best friend, Sabrina Davis, and some of the members of my celibacy club Worth the Wait. As usual, my dad was nowhere to be found.

"Go, Courtland," someone yelled, and the grin I had pasted on my face grew wider even though I didn't think that was possible. I threw them a wink, since I was forbidden to wave, then blocked everything out in order to do our routine.

The music started and I did a mental countdown, then we launched into a series of flips and stunts unlike anything our school had ever seen.

It was my junior year, and as co-captain, I was determined to show the student body of Grover High School in Birmingham, Alabama, that this year's cheerleading squad was going to be different. In the past, squads did these regimented, boring routines that had people in the stands yawning and looking at their watches, ready to get back to the game.

After we had been elected co-captains, my teammate Candy Harris and I, along with our new squad adviser, Coach Wilkins, had agreed it was time for something new. In addition to funky routines, we had decided to compete in regionals, and if we won there, we were gonna try and make it to the national competition in Orlando. We were gonna bring it like it had never been brought before, just like that black squad in that movie *Bring It On,* only better.

The beat of Chris Brown's latest remix featuring Lil' Wayne filled the packed gymnasium, and Candy and I grinned at each other when we saw the audience members smile with delight.

We started breaking it down and the crowd jumped to its feet, cheering us on. The song faded out, and we launched into the cheerleading portion of our routine, doing chants and toe touches that had people slapping high fives at our creativity.

I mentally prepared myself for my backflip, which would land me on top of a five-person pyramid. When a roar ran through the crowd, I made the mistake of looking up just as my secret crush, basketball phenom and star forward Allen Benson, started working the stands, slapping hands and bumping shoulders with everyone within his reach.

I took in his neat cornrows, the sexy tattoo on his bicep and his dimpled smile just as I took off running. Before I could stop myself, I tripped and went rolling like a bowling ball into my teammates, toppling the well-constructed pyramid.

Oooh, the crowd groaned.

By the time I was helped up from the bottom of the pile, laughter surrounded me and my honey-brown face was tinged with embarrassment. I had never been so mortified in all my sixteen years.

I tried to smile and keep eye contact with the crowd, but my face was flaming, and it seemed like Allen was staring right at me.

I tugged at my short cheerleader skirt, trying to cover my thighs, then reminded myself I wasn't the overweight girl I had been two years ago, which still didn't help my embarrassment.

As we were heading back to the locker room, I immediately started apologizing.

"I'm sorry, guys," I said. "I don't know what happened."

"You should be," Rene White said. She was my least favorite squad member because she always found the negative in everything. "Obviously you didn't know the routine as well as you thought you did. You had us out there looking crazy. I can't believe you are co-captain. You can't lead yourself. How are you gonna help lead a squad?"

I started to roll my eyes at her, but changed my mind when I saw our team adviser, Coach Wilkins, headed our way.

"Give her a break," Candy said. "Accidents happen."

I knew she was just trying to be nice. I saw the disappointment in her eyes, even though she looked away to try and hide it.

"Yeah, you'd have messed up, too, if you were about to do a backflip and Allen Benson walked in," one of the other squad members said.

A few of the girls laughed, and I tried to join in, but I was faking.

We made our way back to the sideline just as our archenemies, the Baldwin Eagles, finished their routine. I took a few minutes to glance at Allen again. He was looking really sexy in a pair of jeans and a T-shirt that revealed his muscles. He smiled at someone, and my heart sped up when I saw the dimple in his right cheek. One of his friends said something to him, and he looked in my direction.

My heart skipped a beat. I smoothed my hair and tried to play it cool until he burst out laughing. I tugged at my top, trying to cover my belly, knowing he was laughing at me.

"You guys were terrible," a voice said, and I stopped focusing on myself long enough to stare at the girl who had spoken. It was Emily Arrington, a member of the Baldwin squad.

"It was just a homecoming show," I said. "We'll beat you at regionals."

"Don't count on it," she said, tossing her shiny blond hair. Her butt was bigger than a lot of black girls I knew, and she didn't have any problems shaking what her momma gave her whenever she had the chance.

"Is that a threat?" I asked.

"No, it's a promise," she said, getting in my face like she was going to do something, then walking away.

"You know she's right," Rene said. I saw her mouth moving, but I didn't hear the rest of what she was saying because at that moment, Allen Benson was walking toward me.

"Hey, Courtland," he said, giving me a sexy grin.

I gulped, shocked he knew my name.

"Hey," I squeaked out.

"Are you okay? I was really worried when I saw you fall."

"I'm cool," I said, glancing at the floor and hoping my cheeks weren't as red as they felt.

"Hey, I was wondering if you wanted to get together sometime."

I looked up at him in surprise, then gulped and tucked my hair behind my ear. "Okay," I said.

"Why don't you give me your number, and I'll call you later?"

He had just reached for his cell phone when suddenly a stray football came flying toward me. I tried to catch it, but I stumbled over someone's football helmet and landed on my butt.

My life just couldn't get any worse.

"Courtland, Momma said get up so we aren't late for school," my eight-year-old sister, Cory, said, shaking me awake. "Why are you on the floor?"

"What?" I said. I glanced up at my messy bed then down at my pillow, which was clutched in my arms like a football. I had been in the middle of the best and worst dream of my life, and Cory had just ruined it.

"Come on," she said. "We don't want to be late."

I groaned, until I realized what day it was.

It was the first day of junior year, and I was so excited it had taken me forever to fall asleep the night before. I had been waiting for this year for what seemed like all my life.

In a few short months—Christmas Day, to be exact— I, Courtland Murphy, would turn seventeen and be able to date. Most of my friends had started dating when they were fifteen or sixteen, and although I had begged my mother, she insisted I had plenty of time for boys and that I had to wait until I was seventeen.

Since I had started Grover High School, I had become pretty well known, but I was still getting used to my popularity. I had been overweight the entire time I was in junior high school, and the summer before freshman year, I had decided to make a change. I had started working out, and by the time school started, I had lost twenty pounds and grown a couple of inches.

There were only a handful of kids at Grover who had attended junior high school with me, and a couple of them didn't even recognize me on the first day. I hadn't expected that, or for guys to be checking me out. Honestly, I still wasn't used to the attention, although I'm not gonna lie, I enjoy it. Who wouldn't want fine guys speaking to them?

A couple had asked me out, but since I couldn't date, I had to pretend I wasn't interested. I had gotten a reputation of being stuck-up, but I had decided all that was going to change this year as soon as my birthday rolled around.

Being a cheerleader had given me a chance to meet a lot of the hottest athletes at school, and being co-captain this year was just the thing I needed to get me one step closer to hooking up with Allen Benson, the finest guy at Grover—actually in the state of Alabama.

I had landed a place on the varsity cheerleading squad two years before—the only freshman to do so—and our squad had come a long way over the past two years.

Cheerleading wasn't really my thing. I had been a member of the peewee squad when I was little, and even though I was overweight back then, I was good at it. I had stopped when I started junior high, but once I got to high school, Momma encouraged me to try out, saying it would help me make friends.

I didn't really think I had a shot at making the squad since it's pretty competitive, but to my surprise I had. It wasn't until we were halfway through the season that our old cheerleading adviser, Ms. Caldwell, let it slip in front of everyone she and Momma used to be best friends in high school, and that's how I had ended up on the team. Thank God she moved to Michigan at the end of last school year.

I started to quit, but instead I figured I had to show my squad members that I deserved to be there. I spent the whole summer before sophomore year training, and my hard work paid off. Not only was I an even better cheerleader, thanks to my workouts, I was sporting six-pack abs that put the singer Ciara to shame.

My father didn't like the fact that I wore those short cheerleader skirts and that we had a couple of guys on the squad who often had to lift me, but I figured that was his problem. It's not like he had ever seen me cheer since I started high school. He was never home—usually working at the police precinct—but Momma and Cory were at every game.

I checked my purse to make sure I had the essentials—pen, lip gloss and money—then grabbed my backpack, pom-poms and a change of clothes for cheerleading practice, and I headed downstairs. As always, Momma had a hot breakfast waiting for me and Cory. She was the secretary at our church, First Baptist, Morning Heights, and it kept her busy, as did running around with me and my sister. Cory wasn't as involved in extracurricular activities as me. She had tried sports for a while because Daddy wanted her to, but she quit after the first soccer game. She hated the way Daddy yelled at her from the sidelines, and I guess I couldn't blame her. It had been horrible. People were staring at Daddy like he was crazy, and at one point the referee had even threatened to kick him out. He had calmed down a little, but Cory had still been embarrassed, and she refused to play again. Momma had signed her up for tae kwon do, and she was active in the Girls Scouts at our church, so she was happy.

Daddy wasn't. He was a total athlete in high school and college, and he didn't like the fact that he only had girls. I was supposed to be a boy, and Momma said he was so excited when he found out she was pregnant.

My aunt Dani told me once that Daddy was sad for days after he found out I was a girl. He still wanted to pretend I was a boy for a long time. I remember he used to spend time with me, taking me to play basketball and doing other stuff together. We grew up really close, and I became his shadow, following him everywhere. That all changed the summer before freshman year. He would promise to spend time with me then never show up, so after a while, I stopped expecting anything from him. I really liked basketball, and when I was little I used to dream of playing for the WNBA. I got so sick of Daddy riding me that I pretended to lose interest so he'd leave me alone. I figured cheerleading would at least get me close to sports, but it wasn't really the same.

When Cory came along, I got to witness for myself how excited Daddy was about having a boy. When she turned out to be a girl, too, he was depressed for weeks, and I started to realize being a girl wasn't good enough. He made it seem like Cory and I were such disappointments to him, all because we were girls, something we had no control over.

Daddy still couldn't understand why we weren't interested in all things sports.

Momma was the total opposite. Although she was strict, she wanted us to pursue whatever interested us, and she supported us wholeheartedly, shuttling us back and forth to practices and meetings and attending all our events. The only thing she insisted upon was that we be active in church, which I didn't mind because First Baptist has a fantastic youth department. We are always doing something—

plays, dances, trips to Six Flags in Georgia or Alabama Adventure amusement park—and I really enjoyed Bible study every Wednesday night, as well as our celibacy club, Worth the Wait, which met every other week.

"Good morning, Momma," I said, planting a kiss on her cheek. She was standing at the stove flipping pancakes, and she turned to me and smiled.

"Hey, Miss Junior," she said. "How does it feel?"

"Good," I said, taking a seat at the table next to Cory, whose eyes were glued to her Game Boy—did I mention she's addicted to it? "It will feel even better when we win regionals and after my first date."

Momma rolled her eyes. Every chance I got, I mentioned dating so she didn't forget her promise I could start going out once I turned seventeen.

"What time does cheerleading practice end?" she asked, sliding a plate of pancakes, bacon and cheese eggs in front of me and my sister. She put a plate in front of her seat then grabbed the Game Boy from Cory, who protested loudly, but Momma ignored her as she turned it off and sat across from us. She grabbed our hands, which was our signal to say grace.

After blessing the food, we dug in.

"Where's Daddy?" I asked.

"He had to leave early," she said a bit too quickly.

I nodded. I saw a sadness in Momma's eyes, so I tried to cheer her up.

"Practice ends at five," I said, "but once you get me my Aviator, that won't be a problem since I'll be able to drive myself wherever I need to go." I had gotten my license, but it was rare Momma let me drive. She said she worried too much with me behind the wheel.

As expected, Momma smiled. The Lincoln Aviator was my dream car, and although we both knew I wasn't getting it for my birthday, we liked to joke about it anyway.

"I probably won't be there until five-thirty since your sister has Scouts after school today. Don't you have a Worth the Wait meeting tonight?"

I nodded as I swallowed a mouthful of eggs. "That's cool," I said. "By the time I shower and change, it will be about that time anyway. Worth the Wait meeting is at six-thirty."

Our church had started Worth the Wait last year and Momma had insisted I join. There were actually more members there than I had expected, but I quickly learned half of the girls were there because their moms made them join, too. Only a handful of us were virgins, and although I planned to save myself for marriage, I had started off thinking that was my business, and I didn't make a point of advertising it. But over the last year, hearing all about the AIDS epidemic and the rise in syphilis outbreaks in Alabama and seeing all these baby mommas had made still having my virginity something I was proud of. I made it a point to recruit people whenever I could. I wanted other kids to know that being a virgin was nothing to be ashamed of.

Our adviser, Andrea Mitchell, was cool. She was only twenty-eight, but she offered good advice, and she wasn't ashamed to let the world know she was celibate. Notice

I said celibate and not a virgin. She told us she had had sex once and decided it wasn't worth it, and she had been celibate ever since. After prayer and Bible study, we spent a lot of our meetings role-playing how to stay out of heated situations, but eventually we always ended up talking about sex. We all made a point to bring articles and stuff about abstinence and second virginity for those that had slipped up and had sex and wanted to reclaim their virginity.

We all had these necklaces with one pearl to symbolize that our virginity was as precious as a pearl, and Andrea was talking about having a purity ball next year where we would be presented with purity rings and sign purity pacts, vowing to stay celibate until marriage. She had also been encouraging us to invite people of different races to our meetings, and she said it would be nice to invite some guys, too.

I thought about inviting Allen to a meeting and started giggling so hard I choked on a piece of bacon.

"You okay?" Momma asked, whacking me on the back and looking concerned.

I nodded, took a sip of juice, then turned to my sister, who had been really quiet. "So, munchkin, you happy about starting third grade?"

"I guess," she said, shrugging as she played with her food. Cory was only eight, but she was small for her age. She wore glasses, and they seemed to take up most of her face.

"What's wrong?" Momma asked, frowning.

"What if I don't know any of the kids?" she asked.

Momma put down her fork and grabbed her hand. "Oh, honey, I'm sure it will be most of the same kids who were in your class last year."

"Yeah, and if not, you'll just make new friends," I said.

Cory looked at her plate. "But I don't make friends as easy as you," she said.

"That's not true. You forget I'm shy, too," I said, feeling sorry for her. "It just takes you a little longer. It's going to be fine, okay?"

"Okay," she finally said.

My little sister was really shy, and she was right, she didn't make friends easily. She liked to sit back and observe people. I used to be the same way. I still saw myself as the fat kid, and when I saw people staring, I always secretly wondered if they were thinking I looked like a cow or something. Being a cheerleader had given me more confidence, so I was just reaching the point where I could walk into a room and start talking. Regardless, Cory is the sweetest girl I know. Even though she's my little sister, I enjoy spending time with her. She is really pretty hilarious once she gets going, and not many people know it, but she can dance her butt off. I think by the time she's my age and fills out a little, guys are going to go crazy over her.

Momma glanced at the clock. "You guys ready?" she asked, taking a final sip of coffee.

I took another bite of my pancakes and pushed back my chair. "I am," I said.

Cory just stood without saying anything.

We scraped our plates, rinsed them off and put them in the sink, then we grabbed our stuff and headed out to Momma's Honda Pilot.

"Can I drive today?" I asked.

Momma looked like she was going to say no, so I quickly said, "Daddy won't let me drive his car, so the only time I get to do it is when I'm with you. Please?"

Momma sighed and handed over the keys. "Be careful," she cautioned.

I nodded and ran around to the driver's side. After we were buckled in, I adjusted the rearview mirror, then slowly backed out of the driveway. As I stopped at the sign at the end of our street, Daddy turned the corner. I glanced over at Momma, and she was frowning.

I blew the horn and let down the window. "Hey, Daddy," I said.

"Hey," he said gruffly. He looked like he had just rolled out of bed, and from the looks of it, he had on the same shirt he had worn the day before.

We sat there in silence for a few seconds. When the awkwardness finally got to me, I said, "Well, we're going to be late." I rolled up the window before he could respond and drove off.

I glanced over at Momma again, but she was staring out the window. Cory was busy playing her Game Boy, which she had grabbed off the counter before we left, so I turned on the radio. I really wanted to listen to 95.7 Jamz, but I knew Momma liked gospel, so I turned it to Heaven 610 for her. They were playing Birmingham's first

American Idol Ruben Studdard's version of "Amazing Grace," and Momma looked at me and smiled.

We dropped off Cory at Epic, which is a school for really smart kids, then Momma and I headed to Grover, which was a few blocks away on the south side.

"What do you have planned today?" I asked, just to make conversation.

"Just working and taking care of you kids," she said with a shrug.

She just looked so sad to me. "Why don't we have a girls-only day on Saturday? I only have two more free weekends before football season starts. We can go get manicures and pedicures," I said.

Momma brightened a little. "That'll be fun," she said. "Dani will be here—"

"Aunt Dani's coming to town?" I asked, getting excited.

My aunt, Loretta Danielle Dennis, is twenty-one, only three and a half years older than me, so she's really like my big sister. She and Momma are half sisters, and they are nothing alike. Momma is all about church and taking care of us kids; Aunt Dani wouldn't be caught dead in a church. She spends every weekend partying, and she has no problem living off all the men she dates. Daddy says she's a bad influence, but I love hanging with her whenever she comes to town. She's been living in L.A. the last few years, pursuing modeling and dating this music producer named Triple T. Before that, she lived in New York with her mother.

She e-mails me every now and then telling these crazy

stories about hanging out with celebrities and all these modeling gigs she's gotten.

Her last e-mail a few weeks ago said she had gotten the lead in a national hamburger commercial. I stayed up three days trying to catch it, excited to see my aunt on TV. It wasn't until I saw this ad for, like, the tenth time that I realized Aunt Dani was in it. I didn't recognize her because she was wearing a hamburger costume.

"She said she'll be here later today. I'll call her when I get to work."

"Okay," I said, really looking forward to it.

We rode the last few minutes to school in silence. I wanted to ask Momma if everything was okay with her and Daddy, but past experience had taught me that it was none of my business. When we finally arrived, I leaned over and gave Momma a kiss. "Have a great day," I said. "I love you."

Momma looked at me and smiled, and her espresso-brown eyes lit up. "I love you, too, baby. You're a really good daughter," she said.

"And you're a great mother."

"Thank you. I needed to hear that," she said.

I wanted to ask her what she meant by that, but before I could, my best friend, Sabrina Davis, ran over to the driver's side and called out, "Courtland, come on." She looked past me at Momma. "Hey, Mrs. Murphy."

"Good morning, Bree," Momma said, and just like that, the moment was gone. "Have a good day, baby."

I nodded and grabbed my things from the backseat.

Momma walked around to the driver's side and quickly got in and drove away. I watched her, wondering if she was really okay since she normally waited until Cory and I were safely inside the building before she drove off.

"You coming?" Bree asked.

"Yeah," I said.

We hurried to the auditorium where we sat through the boring first-day orientation where the principal reviewed the do's and don'ts of the school. Since I had heard the same speech the last two years, I tuned him out and gazed around the auditorium, wondering if I would spot any new faces. I checked out the other juniors and seniors first, since I had no interest in dating freshmen or sophomores, but everyone pretty much looked the same. A few people waved, and I waved back, amazed at some of the transformations that had taken place over the summer. Girls had gotten breasts and some had to have bought some hair because there is no way they had grown all that in a few months. Some of the boys were now sporting facial hair, and a few of them were looking kind of good. I wondered which would have the pleasure of being the first guy to date me, and as though in answer to my thoughts, a commotion started at the back of the room.

Bree and I turned to see what was going on. Walking down the aisle as though he was right on time was Allen Benson, and he was much finer than I remembered—he looked even better than he did in my dream. He had been on television a couple of times during the summer, but I hadn't seen him face-to-face since the last day of school. Just the sight of him made a chill run down my spine.

Allen was a senior, and he was the star basketball player at Grover. Word had it that he was going pro rather than going to college, and I had to admit he had skills. Allen could play some ball—and he looked mighty good in that blue and gold basketball uniform.

I felt Bree nudging me, and I nodded, indicating I had seen him. How could I miss him? Allen was about six-two, at least six inches taller than me, and he was fine. He had brown skin, kind of like the color of caramel, and he had exchanged his cornrows from last year for a low-cut fade, which made him look even sexier.

As he got closer to our seats, which were about a fourth of the way from the front of the room since the juniors sat right behind the seniors, I patted my hair, which I had in a bob that touched my shoulders. For cheerleading practice, I could just throw it up in a ponytail, which was great. I straightened my empire-cut purple-printed tunic and checked my feet, which were encased in high-heeled sandals, to make sure they weren't ashy, and thankfully they weren't. There was a piece of lint on my purple Capris, and I quickly picked it off, wondering why I was going through all the trouble since he couldn't see the bottom half of me anyway.

When Allen made it to our row, I thought about speaking, but before I could, our principal called, "Mr. Benson, thank you for gracing us with your presence. If you could kindly take your seat, I would appreciate it."

Allen lifted his chin in response, but he didn't move any faster, and the students continued to whisper in awe. After he was finally settled, our principal continued his presentation, introducing all the teachers, the cafeteria workers and maintenance staff.

I grew bored again, so I pulled out my schedule, which Bree and I had picked up on our way in, trying to make sure I knew where I was supposed to go after homeroom.

I glanced at the paper and frowned.

"What's wrong?" Bree asked, leaning forward to peer at the schedule.

"They have me listed in the wrong English class," I said. "I'm not supposed to take African-American lit until next semester."

Bree shrugged. "It's probably just a mistake," she said. "Do we have any classes together?" We had been so busy catching up with our friends before coming into the auditorium that we hadn't even bothered to check.

It turned out we had lunch and dance class together, which I found funny since Bree was definitely not the dance type. She tripped over her own feet with every other step she took.

"Why'd you sign up for dance?" I asked, noticing our principal was finally wrapping up.

"The only other options were band, PE or ROTC. Can you see me doing any of those?" she asked.

"Good point," I said. "Well, I'll just help you with the dances."

"Of course you will," she said. "Just like I'll help you with math."

"Whatever," I said, and we laughed. We were both straight-A students.

Bree and I had known each other since fifth grade, but it wasn't until freshman year that we really clicked. We had both gotten stuck taking band for some reason, and we spent a lot of time talking about ourselves and our families. We got to know each other really well, and I told her pretty much everything. Whereas I was into sports, Bree was more creative. She was on the yearbook staff, and she was a regular contributor to the school newspaper and creative-writing magazine.

"Where are you headed after homeroom?" she asked, as kids began to gather their things so they could leave.

"I'm supposed to go to English, but I have to straighten out my schedule first," I said.

"Cool. Well, I guess I'll see you at lunch," she said.

I nodded and waved.

I almost didn't make it to homeroom on time because kids kept stopping me to say hello. I slid into my seat just as the bell rang, then listened to another long list of instructions before our teacher, Ms. Ross, passed out cards for us to fill out our emergency information. Once that was done, I asked her if I could leave early to get my schedule changed, and she agreed.

It turned out to be a waste of my time since all the other classes were full.

English class was just about to start when I walked in, so I dropped in the first seat I saw, which happened to be at the front of the room. I grabbed a pen from my purse, and just as I was uncapping the pen, the top flew off. I reached down to get it and bumped heads with someone who was also reaching for it.

"Thank you," I said, looking up for the first time. My heart went into overdrive because staring back at me was Allen Benson. "What are you doing here?" I asked before I could stop myself.

He laughed, and I blushed.

"I didn't mean that the way it sounded," I said. "It's just that this is a junior class, and you're a senior."

"Thanks for reminding me," he joked.

"You don't like being a senior?" I asked. That's all Bree and I talked about. The seniors ruled the school, and with that title came a world we could only dream about—dating, driving, prom, applying to college.

"Not when I have to double up on my English classes since I failed this one last year. If I want to graduate, I've got to take them both."

"Why didn't you just go to summer school?" I asked, not believing I was talking with Allen Benson—the Allen Benson.

"I was in basketball camps all summer," he said, "so I couldn't go."

"I wasn't supposed to take this class until next semester, but I think it'll be fun. I love reading."

"I might have to get you to tutor me," he said.

"Not a problem," I said, hoping I sounded confident, although inside I was sweating at the thought of spending time alone with him.

I stuck out my hand. "I'm Courtland Murphy, and you are?"

He gave a little laugh and engulfed his paw around my hand. "Cute. I'm Allen Benson. Nice to meet you, Miss Courtland. By the way, I like your outfit."

Before I could respond, our teacher started class. "Good morning, students. I hope you all had a great summer."

Ms. Watters glanced around the room, which was decorated in pink and green. "I see many of you remember my rules from last year." I looked around in confusion, and Ms. Watters explained, "Wherever you sit on the first day of school is where you sit the entire semester."

I groaned to myself. I hated sitting in the very front of the room since it made me an easy target for getting called on. It's not that I didn't know the answers—usually I did—but I didn't want kids to think I was as smart as I was. I had been teased enough for that in elementary school. I glanced over at Allen, and he was smiling at me.

"Did you know what she was going to do?" I asked when Ms. Watters went to her desk. He nodded. "So, why'd you sit in the front?"

"I figured if I was up here, maybe I'd pass the class."

I nodded in understanding before I focused on Ms. Watters, who had started passing out the syllabus for the semester. It was printed on pink and green paper, and I assumed she was a member of Alpha Kappa Alpha sorority, which was confirmed when I spotted an AKA mug on her desk. As I took a sheet and passed the rest of the stack back, Allen slid me a piece of notebook paper.

I tried to pretend I wasn't fazed as I waited for Ms. Watters to get to the other side of the room before I opened it.

I GUESS YOU'RE STUCK WITH ME, it read, and I couldn't help but smile. I had never looked forward more to an English class in my life.

When I met Bree for lunch, I was still carrying around Allen's note like it was a Grammy award.

"Girl," I said the minute I spotted her, "you will never guess who's in my English class." I grabbed her arm and dragged her to the cafeteria line where Bree got a burger and fries and I picked up a salad. I didn't even get annoyed for the thousandth time that Bree could eat whatever she wanted without gaining weight.

"Are you going to tell me?" Bree asked, getting excited.

"I can show you better than I can tell you," I said as we made our way to our table. We put down our trays, and I grabbed my purse and pulled out my wallet where I had safely tucked Allen's note. I passed it to Bree, who struggled to read the tiny writing.

"Who's it from?" she asked after finally deciphering it.

"Guess," I said.

"Courtland," Bree wailed, "just tell me."

I pretended to shoot a basket, and after a second Bree caught on. "No," she said, her eyes growing wide.

I nodded and grinned. "Yes," I said.

"Allen Benson gave this to you?" she squealed.

I didn't say a word as I added dressing to my salad.

"Girl, I am so jealous. Tell me everything, and don't leave out any details."

I hadn't gotten far before other members of Worth the Wait and some of the cheerleaders descended on the table. I gave Bree a look, letting her know I'd fill her in later. It's not that I didn't trust my other friends, but I didn't want to take any chances that people would be hating on me. I had been around enough females in general to know that they were messy and always looking for something to gossip about, so I kept my business to myself. That's something my momma had always told me, that whatever happened at home stayed there.

I looked at Allen's note about a hundred times more before school ended, and I thought about it through most of cheerleading practice although I nailed my toe touches and basket tosses. I guess Allen was training for basketball season because he was running around the track and looking so good in a pair of black shorts and a white T-shirt. He was drenched in sweat, which only made him look sexier. All the girls on the squad were talking about him, and I couldn't blame them.

As I was waiting for Momma to pick me up after practice, I looked at Allen's note again and smiled to myself, thinking how crazy it would be if we ended up dating. I couldn't help but laugh at the thought. There was no way Allen could be interested in me.

I glanced at my watch and noticed it was almost six o'clock. I realized I hadn't checked to see if Momma had left a message for me during practice, so I retrieved my phone.

Allen caught me off guard for the second time that day.

"You must have been reading my mind," he said,

causing me to drop my phone. He laughed as he picked it up and handed it to me. "I didn't mean to scare you."

"It's okay," I said, holding on to the phone as tightly as I could with my slippery hands. "So how was I reading your mind?"

"When I saw you while I was running, I realized I didn't ask for your number during class. I was just thinking that if I saw you I was going to ask for it."

I had stopped breathing when he said *number.* "My phone number?" I squeaked.

"Yeah," he said, "if that's okay. I figured I need to have you on speed dial just in case I have a question about class."

I tried not to let my disappointment show. He just wanted help with English. "Sure," I said. "If you have a phone, I can program my number in for you."

He shook his head. "I'd rather you write it down. That way, if my phone breaks, I'll still have it."

"Okay," I said, trying not to read anything into what he was saying. This was strictly about school, I kept telling myself, but obviously my stomach wasn't listening because it was doing flips like it was competing for the Olympic gold medal in gymnastics. I grabbed a notebook and a pen out of my bag and scribbled down my number.

"Give me your e-mail address, too," he said.

I nodded and added it to the sheet, then tore it out of my notebook and handed it to him.

"I'll be in touch," he said, folding the paper. He grabbed a set of keys from his gym bag, which was slung across his shoulder. "Hey, do you need a ride?"

Of course I wanted to say yes, but I knew Momma and Daddy would have a fit if I got in the car with a boy, so I played it off. "Nah, I'm cool. My ride will be here in a minute."

"I don't bite," he said, and I laughed.

"I know," I said, twirling my Worth the Wait necklace, which I sometimes did when I got nervous. "Maybe I'll take you up on that offer some other time."

"Maybe you should," Allen said, stepping a little closer to me. I felt his breath on my cheek, and my heart sped up.

"That's a nice necklace," he said. "Did your man give it to you?"

I laughed. "Actually, it's my purity necklace," I said before I could stop myself. I blushed and looked at the ground, then glanced up at him to see his response.

"Really?" he asked, raising an eyebrow.

I shrugged. "Yeah. My mom had me join this virgin club at my church, and each of the members got one of these necklaces."

"I've heard about those clubs. I know a few other girls here are members. When did you join?"

"Last year," I said. "I recruited some of the girls from school." Allen made me feel so comfortable that I told him a few more details about Worth the Wait, and he seemed really impressed.

"So can guys join?" he asked.

"Sure. It's open to anyone who wants to take a vow of purity, although our group has mostly teenagers. I can get you more information if you want."

Momma chose that moment to pull up, and, spotting me, she blew her horn and waved. I was so embarrassed. "Is that your mom?" Allen asked.

I nodded, not believing my momma was messing up my game. She pulled up next to us and looked at Allen curiously. He smiled and walked up to her. "Good evening, Mrs. Murphy. My name is Allen Benson. I was just keeping your daughter company while she waited for you."

Momma smiled and shook his hand. "It's nice to meet you, Allen." She stared at him for a second. "Haven't I seen you on TV?"

Allen shyly looked down at the ground. "Yes, ma'am," he said.

"You're making quite a name for yourself, young man. I know your parents are proud."

"They are," he said.

Momma nodded. "And you're keeping up with your studies?"

"Momma," I protested. I couldn't believe how she was grilling him like he was my man or something.

"Actually, that's what I was talking to your daughter about. I got behind in my classes last year, and I'm trying to play catch-up, and I was hoping she could tutor me in English."

"You realize my daughter is only sixteen, and she can't date yet," Momma said, looking him in the eye.

"Oh, no, ma'am," Allen was quick to say, raising his hands and backing away like the thought of dating me repulsed him. "This is strictly about school. I was just telling her that I would call if I had any questions, and if it's okay with you, we can meet in the library during our study period so we can do our homework."

Momma looked at him, trying to figure out if he was playing games. She must have believed him because she said, "I guess that will be fine. I don't know how much you guys will be able to get accomplished during an hour, so if you need to meet with her after school, I guess you could study at our house."

My mouth dropped open in amazement. Other guys had tried to hook up with me, but Momma wasn't impressed. She didn't play when it came to Cory and me.

"Thank you so much, Mrs. Murphy. I really appreciate it. I also want to say that I see where your daughter gets her beauty from."

Momma and I both blushed. Momma recovered first and said, "Allen, you're laying it on a bit too thick now."

"Yes, ma'am," he said, and they both laughed. He turned to me. "I'll see you in school tomorrow, Courtland."

I could only nod and wave as I got in the front seat.

"He's cute and quite the charmer," Momma said the minute we pulled away.

I could only nod at her as Allen waved at us. "Did you really just say he could come over and study—not that he will?"

Momma shrugged. "Why not?" she said. "He seems nice enough, and the Bible tells us to help those in need."

I wasn't going to argue with her, although deep down I

knew that Allen was just being nice. There was no way he would ever want to study with me, let alone visit my house.

"Hey, munchkin," I said to Cory, who was sitting in the backseat. "How was the first day?"

She looked up from her Game Boy and grinned at me. "I made a friend," she said, and I smiled, too, happy for my little sister.

"That's great," I said.

Cory told me about her friend Destini, who she said was in foster care, then we rode to the Worth the Wait meeting in silence. Several of the girls were arriving as we pulled up. A few girls had skipped meetings that summer, and apparently at least one of them had forgotten the pledge to remain pure until she got married because I was pretty sure that wasn't a watermelon she was sporting under her shirt.

I looked at Momma to see if she had noticed, and she shook her head. "Now why would that child's mother still make her attend these meetings?" she said.

"Maybe she's supposed to serve as an example," I said, fingering my pearl necklace, which served as a constant reminder to me that my virginity was a gift, and I wasn't giving it up to anyone but my husband.

My thoughts shifted when there was a knock on my window. I looked up into the grinning face of my aunt Dani and let out a scream as I struggled to get out of the car and hug her.

"Aunt Dani," I yelled, squeezing her tight. I hadn't seen her in three years—she'd come to Birmingham right before moving to L.A.—but she still looked the same. Her breasts were bigger, if that was possible, and she had a ponytail weave that reached her butt and was dyed burgundy at the bottom. Even though it was August and about ninety degrees, she was wearing a black leather short set and black leather boots.

She squeezed me tight. "Corky, is that you?" she asked, stepping back to look at me. "Girl, I'm glad you finally lost all that baby fat. It looks like you're out of your ugly phase, too."

She was talking loud, and people were looking at us as they entered the church.

"I don't go by Corky, Aunt Dani," I said. "Everybody calls me Courtland now."

"Girl, please. You'll always be Corky, just like I'll always be Dani," she said. "Ain't that right, sis?" She looked at Momma, who gave this really tight smile before she and Cory hugged Aunt Dani and headed into church.

"So how long are you in town? Are you staying with us?" I asked.

"I haven't decided," she said. "I'm going to take a break from modeling, so I figured I'd hang with you guys for a while. Girl, you know your house is too small. I have a room at the Sheraton near the Civic Center."

"That's cool," I said, just as our Worth the Wait adviser, Andrea, motioned for me to come inside. "You coming into church?"

Aunt Dani kind of laughed under her breath before walking over to a brand-new BMW SUV. "Nah, I've got some people I need to see. Your mother told me you would be here, so I wanted to stop and say hello." She hit a button on the remote to unlock the doors.

"Is that yours?" I asked.

"Of course," she said, looking at me like I was silly for asking.

I wondered how she'd gotten a car so fast since she had just come to town, but I really didn't care. "I guess modeling is paying well."

"Girl, modeling isn't the only way to get paid."

She must have noticed the confusion on my face because she grinned. "We'll have to get together soon so I can explain the facts of life," she said. Then she was gone.

two

I **was** getting dressed in the locker room before our final practice for the first football game of the season when my cell phone rang.

Since Coach Wilkins was already yelling at us to get on the field, I thought about ignoring it, but at the last minute I changed my mind.

"Hello," I said in a rushed tone.

"Is this a bad time?" a voice said.

"I'm about to go to practice," I said. "Who is this?"

"Who do you want it to be?" he asked.

I rolled my eyes and played along. "Chris Brown, is that you?" I joked, referring to the popular singer.

"Cute," the guy said.

"Seriously, I'm late for practice. If you're not going to tell me who this is, can you call me back in a couple of hours?"

The guy laughed. "It's Allen," he said.

I dropped onto the bench in the locker room. "Hey," I said, trying to sound as though I talked to him on the phone all the time. "How come you weren't in class today?"

"I had to meet with some people," he explained.

"Oh," I said. "You didn't miss much, although we do have a test next Friday."

"I heard," he said. "That's actually why I'm calling."

"What's up?" I said, nodding at Candy, who stuck her head in the locker room and told me to hurry up.

"Can we get together a couple of days next week and study? I really need to do well on this test."

"Sure," I said, telling myself that studying with Allen Benson wasn't such a big deal.

"That's cool. Why don't we meet Monday during study hall?"

"Okay. Have a good weekend. Good luck at the game," he said.

"Thanks," I said. I ended the call then double-checked to make sure I had actually turned the phone off, then I got up and danced around the empty locker room. I was so keyed up I didn't hear Coach Wilkins come in.

"You need to save that energy for the field," she said. "Please feel free to join us whenever you're ready."

I hustled onto the field and went through the motions at practice, too focused on Monday during study hall. I couldn't believe I was actually going to be studying with Allen Benson.

The first game of the season had me pumped. For me, there's nothing like being in front of a crowd. I spotted

Momma and Cory in the stands, and I shook my blue and gold pom-poms at them. They waved back, then I tuned them out, intent on giving my best performance.

I had choreographed a routine to Chamillionaire's latest hit for halftime, and the crowd loved it.

Even though we lost the game, I knew it was going to be a good season for our squad. We were all pumped about regionals and possibly competing at nationals in Orlando.

I had asked Momma before the game if I could go out with the squad, and she had reluctantly agreed, after Aunt Dani talked her into it, telling her I was only going to be young once. I still had to be home by ten-thirty, but I decided not to push my luck. Although I wanted to stay out longer, I couldn't complain because the year before she had barely allowed me to go out.

Candy was driving, so I went and said goodbye to Momma and Cory.

"You sure you don't want me to drive you?" Momma asked, looking worried.

"Momma," I said, dragging out her name like it had ten syllables. "I'm almost seventeen. Candy's a good driver."

She opened her mouth to speak, but before she could, Cory said, "You're treating her like a baby."

I smiled my thanks.

"Well," Momma said, still looking unsure. "You have your cell phone, right?"

"Yes, ma'am," I said, wondering why she had even bothered to get me one. I begged and begged, and finally she had gotten me one of those prepaid ones.

Half the time I couldn't get a signal and sometimes I would check the voice mail and discover I had three or four messages, although the phone never alerted me they had come in.

She reached into her purse and pulled out twenty dollars and handed it to me. "Call me if you have any problems, and here's some money to call a cab if you can't get in touch with me."

I reached for the money, and she snatched it back, forcing me to look at her. "This money is for emergencies only, Courtland. Keep it in a safe place."

"Okay." I wanted to remind her Birmingham didn't have a lot of cabs, and even if it did, it wasn't like twenty dollars could get me home—at least I didn't think it would.

"Ten-thirty, Courtland. Not a minute later," she warned.

I nodded then turned to head into the locker room. When I got to the door, Momma and Cory were still standing there waiting to make sure I made it in safely, just like I knew they would be.

I took a shower and threw on the sweats that matched our uniforms and my Air Force Ones.

About ten of us piled in Candy's Hyundai Sorrento SUV, and we headed to Ruby Tuesday's in Five Points South. As usual it was packed.

I went to the bathroom, and on the way out, I ran into this guy who had wanted to get with me last year. He was fine and all, but every time I talked to him, he was only interested in coming to my house, which wasn't happening.

"So when can I come over?" Noah asked.

I rolled my eyes. "Don't start," I said, trying to get past him.

"I see you're still as stuck-up as ever," he said. "You ain't all that."

I tried to pretend his words didn't hurt, but they did. I decided to ignore him and went back to my friends.

We had just finished eating and were hanging out by the fountain when my phone beeped, letting me know I had a text message. I wondered if it was Momma, but I realized she would call since she didn't know how to send texts.

You're looking sexy in those sweats, the message read.

I laughed, thinking it was one of my teammates being silly. Then I saw Allen's number, which I had programmed in my phone after he called the first time. I looked around and spotted him across the street at Starbucks. He said something to his boys, which included Noah, then headed my way.

"Hey," he said.

"Hey." I pushed my hair behind my ear and started playing with my purity necklace, until I realized what I was doing. I stuck my hands in the pocket of my sweatshirt.

"What are you doing here?" I asked.

He shrugged. "The same thing as you, I guess, just hanging out. You want to go get some coffee or something?"

I wanted to say yes, but I caught a glimpse of the big clock near the fountain and realized if I went with Allen I'd miss curfew. I had just decided I would take my chances when Candy walked up.

"You ready?" she asked.

I smiled my thanks that she didn't mess up my game by telling Allen about my curfew.

"Hey, Candy," Allen said.

"Hey," she said, not even bothering to look at him.

"Oh, it's like that?" he said. "You can't show me no love?" He stretched his arms out, waiting for a hug.

"No, I can't," she said with an attitude. She turned and walked away. "You coming, Courtland?"

"I've got to get up early tomorrow," I said, wondering if my excuse sounded as lame as it felt. "I'll see you at school next week."

I hurried over to Candy. "What was that about?" I asked.

"Trust me, you don't even want to know."

When we pulled up to the house, Daddy's unmarked squad car was in the driveway, which surprised me. Momma said he had been working a lot of overtime lately, but I didn't really believe it.

"I'll see you guys on Monday," I said, as my teammates chorused goodbye.

The house was quiet when I walked in, and for some reason it scared me. Whenever I went out with my friends, Momma waited up for me, and although I pretended I didn't like it, it was something I expected.

"Where you been?" Daddy asked from the darkness of our den.

"I went out with my friends. Didn't Momma tell you?" I asked.

He didn't respond. I heard ice clinking in a glass, and I knew he was drinking. I hated it when he drank.

"Where's Momma?" I asked.

"Somewhere upstairs," he muttered.

"Do you have to go back to work?" I asked, trying to make conversation as I turned on the hallway light.

Daddy and I rarely talked, and when we did, it seemed as though I was always the one initiating the conversation.

"Nah," he said.

"Where's your car?" I asked.

He glanced at me like I was annoying him. "Why?" he asked.

"I was just asking," I said.

"I had an accident, so I have the squad car until I get it fixed."

I didn't even bother to ask if he was okay. "Good night," I said and headed upstairs. Cory was already asleep, and I found Momma in her room reading her Bible.

I knocked on the partially open door. "I'm back," I said.

She smiled. "Did you have a good time?" she asked.

"Yes, ma'am."

"Where'd you guys go?"

I told Momma about my evening, and although I knew she was listening, her mind seemed to be somewhere else.

"You okay?" I finally asked.

"I'm fine, baby," she said.

"What did you and Cory do after the game?"

"Nothing much. I was trying to get ready for church tomorrow. Don't forget we have to be there early for the annual prayer breakfast."

I nodded, trying to hide a yawn.

"Why don't you get to bed? You've had a long day."

"Okay," I agreed. I walked over to give her a hug.

She didn't bother to respond. "Momma, are you okay, really?" I asked, searching her eyes.

She patted my hand. "There's nothing for you to worry about, sweetie. Everything is fine."

"Yes, ma'am," I said. "Good night." I turned to leave then swung back around and gave her a hug. "I love you, Momma."

She squeezed me so hard I thought my ribs would break. "I love you, too, baby."

I got ready for bed, all the while thinking about Momma, trying to figure out why she stayed with Daddy. From what I could see, she didn't love him—I mean they rarely spent time together, and any time Daddy was home, the house was filled with tension. She had a job, so she couldn't use not having money as an excuse. I just didn't understand, and deep down, I didn't want to.

It didn't take me long to get dressed for school Monday morning since I had picked out my outfit the night before. Knowing I was going to see Allen in class every day, I always tried to dress my best, but I went above and beyond this time because I knew we were going to be studying together. I put on a red wrap dress and some red heels and looked at myself in the mirror, realizing I looked like I was trying too hard. I took off the outfit and tried on three more before I finally settled on some jeans and a wrap top and some heels.

I put on some lip gloss and eyeliner, then took off my wrap cap and styled my hair. Finally I added some gold earrings and my purity necklace.

"You look nice," Momma said when I finally made it to the breakfast table. "Anything special going on today?"

"No," I said. "Hey, munchkin."

"Hey," Cory said, glancing up from her Game Boy.

"I was running a little late so I didn't cook," she said apologetically as she set a bowl of oatmeal in front of me.

"It's okay, Momma," I said, digging in after we said grace.

I tuned out the conversation she and Cory were having, focusing instead on my meeting with Allen. By the time I made it to school, I was nervous, but I had no reason to be.

Allen never showed for study hall, and I felt so stupid.

When I met up with Bree for lunch, I tried to play off how much it bothered me, but she knew.

We made small talk all through lunch, and I was just about to dump my tray when Allen walked in. He waved at me like nothing was wrong, but I ignored him. When I heard him calling my name as I walked out the lunch-room door, I thought about not responding. He caught up with me and grabbed my arm, swinging me around.

"I'm so sorry," he said. "I had to meet with Coach Pat-terson, and it ran late."

"Don't worry about it," I said, not bothering to make eye contact with him. Instead I spoke to a few kids who were passing by.

"Courtland, please don't be mad. I promise it won't happen again," he pleaded.

"You could have at least texted me," I said, finally looking at him.

"You're right," Allen said, looking at the floor. He glanced back up at me with a huge smile, showing the dimple in his cheek. "I promise I'll make it up to you."

Seeing the dimple did something to me, and before I knew it, I had forgiven him.

"Just don't let it happen again," I said.

"I won't," he said and he reached down to give me a hug. I closed my eyes, loving the brief moment in his arms. It was better than anything I could dream of—until I spotted the hickey on his neck.

three

I **know** I shouldn't have been mad at Allen. I mean, it's not like he's my man, but seeing that hickey made me so jealous. I wondered if he had been with some other girl when he was supposed to be studying with me, but I didn't ask him because I didn't want him to think I liked him.

"So when do you want to get together?" he asked.

I thought about my schedule for the rest of the week, excited he still wanted to see me. Although I could have made the time, I didn't want him to think he could just see me whenever he wanted. "It looks like you're going to have to study for this test on your own," I said. "I've got to help my best friend with something during study hall and I have cheerleading practice after school for the rest of the week."

We had started learning our first dance routine, and Bree was already behind, so I had promised her I would help her. We could have worked on the dance at my house after school, but I didn't want Allen to think I didn't have a life.

Allen stood looking at me. "I've got to do well on this

test," he said. "I want Ms. Watters to see that I'm serious about passing this class this time. What about if I come over to your house after practice? Your mom said it would be okay," he said.

I laughed. "I think she was just saying that to be polite. I'm not allowed to date yet, so I don't know if she'll really let you come over." I couldn't believe I had told him that instead of pretending I just wasn't interested.

"Well, it's not like it's a date, so it won't hurt to ask her, will it?" Allen said.

I shrugged and looked at the ground since he'd cracked my face. "Why do you want to study with me so bad?" I asked curiously. "I'm sure there are other people who wouldn't mind helping you."

"Yeah, but they're not as cute as you," Allen said.

I couldn't help but blush.

"I'll talk to your mom after school," he said, "and I promise I'll be there on time."

Allen kept his word. He was waiting on me when I got out of practice, and together we walked to my mother's SUV.

"Hey, Mrs. Murphy," he said, bopping up to the driver's side.

"Hi, Allen," she said and gave him a smile that lit up her whole face.

"I was wondering if I could take you up on your offer to study with Courtland. We have a test coming up this week, and I really need her help."

I didn't look at Momma because I didn't want her to

know how much I wanted her to say yes. After what seemed like forever, she finally said, "I guess that will be okay. When would you like to come?"

"How about now?" he said. "If it's okay, I'll ride with you since my car is in the shop. I'll have my dad pick me up later."

I don't think Momma was expecting his response. I know I wasn't.

When Momma agreed, I was about to climb into the backseat so Allen would have room to stretch his long legs, but he told me he'd be fine in the back, so he got in next to Cory, who was, as usual, absorbed in her Game Boy.

I was nervous the entire ride home, trying to remember if I had made up my bed. Then I relaxed, realizing Allen would be in the kitchen and maybe the den, both of which were spotless, just like the rest of the house. I still couldn't believe Allen was headed to my house to sit at my kitchen table and study.

I glanced over at Momma, and she winked at me, and I couldn't help but grin. She patted my leg, indicating I needed to chill. I turned on the radio, and when I heard Momma's favorite gospel station, I went to change it, figuring Allen liked 95.7 Jamz.

"Do you mind leaving it? I love that song," he said as Donnie McClurkin sang his latest hit.

Momma glanced at him in the rearview mirror. "Do you attend church, Allen?" she asked.

I was so embarrassed. I couldn't believe Momma was questioning Allen Benson about his salvation. The guy was too busy playing basketball to have time for God.

"Yes, ma'am," he said. "My dad and I are very active—in fact my dad is a deacon at our church. I play basketball for the church's team, and I help out with the younger kids when I have time."

Momma nodded in approval, and I have to admit I was pleasantly surprised.

"What does your mother do?" she asked.

"My mom used to teach high school English in Hoover," he said. He had this expression like he'd been busted.

"Really?" Momma said with interest.

I turned to him. "So if your mom's an English teacher, why do you need my help?" I asked.

Momma glanced at him in the rearview mirror, also awaiting his response.

"My parents are divorced, and I live with my dad. My mother doesn't like to get involved with my schoolwork," he said. "She said since teachers teach different ways she doesn't want to mess up the way I'm being taught at school." He shrugged and focused on Cory's Game Boy, pointing out something on the screen.

"That was a real slick answer, Allen," Momma said. She tried to be stern, but I could tell she wanted to laugh.

He grinned at her, showing his dimple again, and I wanted to melt. For the first time, I started to wonder if maybe he was coming to my house because he actually wanted to spend time with me, even though he said it wasn't a date. I decided not to let myself focus on that thought.

Daddy's car was in the driveway when we got home,

and I saw an annoyed look pass over Momma's face. It happened so fast, I wondered if I had imagined it.

"Your father's home," she announced, although I wasn't sure why since it was obvious he was there.

We piled out of the car, and Allen offered to get the groceries Momma had put in the back, and I hung around to help.

"I see someone around here likes to hoop," Allen said. He nodded at the basketball rim attached to our garage.

"I fool around every now and then," I said.

"You do?" he asked, sounding surprised.

"Yeah."

"This I've got to see."

"Just name the time and place," I said.

We walked in the back door as Momma was opening the door. She immediately shouted, "Corwin, we're home. We have company."

I wondered what was up since we normally didn't say anything when Daddy was home. He said he hated all the noise we made when we walked through the door, so Cory and I usually headed up to our rooms when he was there.

"Anybody hungry?" Momma asked, glancing nervously toward the den, which is where Daddy normally hung out.

Allen made himself comfortable at our kitchen table like he sat there all the time.

"Yes, ma'am," he said, rubbing his six-pack.

Momma glanced at me, and I had to tear my eyes away from Allen's stomach, which he had exposed when he rubbed it. "What about you, Courtland?"

"Uh, sure," I said. I jumped up from the table before my thoughts got me in trouble. "Do you need some help?" I asked.

Allen got up, too. "What can we do?" he said.

I didn't want to admit how much I liked the sound of that word *we*. It felt like my heart started doing dance moves in my chest.

Cory continued to sit at the table playing her game, and Allen popped her on her head. "Girl, get up and help your momma," he scolded.

Cory jumped up, ready to do whatever Allen asked. I'm sure if Allen had thrown a bone Cory would have gone to fetch it. Actually, I probably would have, too.

"All of you, sit down," Momma said. We did as she asked. "Allen, I'm glad to see your parents raised you right. Maybe you can help me whip these lazy bums into shape," she joked.

"No problem," he said, stretching out his long legs under the table.

Momma got busy fixing us a snack, and Allen, Cory and I opened our books so we could study. She placed a plate of cut-up apples and caramel dip along with some plates in the center of the table, and we dug in.

"Man, this is better than those Apple Dippers from McDonald's," Allen said. "Thanks, Mrs. M."

I smiled at the nickname, and reminded myself to remember everything that happened from the moment I saw Allen so I could tell Bree.

"You're welcome, dear," she said, patting his shoulder.

"Why don't you call your dad to see if you can stay for dinner? I'm making fried chicken—"

"Trust me, you want to stay," Cory said. "My momma makes the best fried chicken in the whole world."

Allen nodded. "Thanks for the heads-up." He turned to Momma. "Are you sure it won't be a problem?"

"Not at all," she said. "We're happy to have you. After you make the pros, I can brag I had someone in the NBA sitting at my kitchen table."

We all laughed.

"What's so funny?" Daddy asked, appearing in the doorway.

I had forgotten he was there. When he walked into the room, the whole atmosphere changed. I prayed he wasn't going to do or say anything stupid.

Daddy turned his gaze on Allen. "What are you doing in my house? My daughter isn't allowed to date," he said.

I couldn't believe he was being so rude. When I was in elementary and junior high, my friends used to love hanging at our house because they all thought my parents were so cool. The summer before ninth grade that all changed, though. Daddy had been on the force about ten years then, and a pregnant woman had been killed during a hostage situation at a bank. I overheard Momma tell a member of our church Daddy felt bad because he had promised her that she would be okay only minutes before the bank robber shot her. After that, Daddy changed. He started drinking more, and he was grumpy all the time. Whenever he was home, it was uncomfortable for all of us.

Allen didn't seem fazed. He stood and walked over to Daddy, towering over him by about three inches. "Hi, Mr. Murphy. My name is Allen Benson. Your daughter is tutoring me in English."

"I know who you are. I don't want you in my house."

"Corwin," Momma said, shocked at his words, although I don't know why.

"It's okay, Mrs. M.," Allen said. "If I had a daughter as beautiful as Courtland, I'd be trying to protect her, too." He gathered his English book and put it in his backpack, and I wondered how he was planning on getting home. "Is it okay if we study together at school? I'm interested in dating your daughter, sir, but I promise you I'll wait until she's seventeen. Until then, I really would appreciate it if you would allow us to study together. I don't know if you know it, but I want to go pro at the end of the school year, and I need your daughter's help to make that happen."

Everyone in the kitchen was silent as we all looked at Daddy. I was staring at him, but I was more focused on the fact that Allen wanted to date me.

"You can stay," Daddy finally muttered. "At least here we can keep an eye on you." He walked out of the room and Allen took a seat at the table. When I looked at him, he winked at me.

Momma seemed to relax a little. Allen went to call his dad, and Momma started making dinner. When Allen returned, he, Cory and I sat there studying.

When we finished, Momma said we had about twenty minutes before dinner.

"You up for a little one on one?" Allen asked.

"You ain't said nothing but a word," I said, sounding like Aunt Dani. "Momma, we'll be back. Let me go whip this boy real quick."

"Oh, it's like that?" Allen asked.

I just smiled.

We both still had on our practice clothes, so I grabbed a ball from the garage and we headed to the driveway. "Let's play to twenty," I said, passing the ball to him.

It took me a second to get in my groove since I hadn't played in a while, but once I did I showed Allen no mercy. He ended up winning twenty to nineteen, but it was a good game.

"Girl, where'd you learn to play like that?" he asked.

I shrugged. "I don't know," I said. "I guess I've just got skills."

He laughed.

"Courtland, dinner's ready," Cory said from the garage.

"Okay."

We walked in just as Momma was finishing up.

"Courtland," she said, spooning mashed potatoes into a serving bowl, "why don't you show Allen where the bathroom is so he can wash up?"

"Okay," I agreed.

I led him down the hall to our guest bathroom and stood in the doorway as he washed his hands.

"So did you really mean what you said earlier?" I asked, my stomach tightening at how he might respond.

"Said about what?" he asked. I thought he was serious until I saw his dimple appear.

I popped him on the arm. "Why are you teasing me?" I asked.

"You thought I really wanted to come over here just to study?" he said.

"Yeah," I admitted. "You said this wasn't a date. Besides, I'm just a junior."

"Well, I want to date you," he said. He looked like he wanted to kiss me, but then he changed his mind.

"Why?" I asked, really wanting to know.

"Because I think you're something special. I've been checking you out since last year, but I didn't know how to approach you. Word is that you're stuck-up, but I know now that's just a cover."

"Really?" I asked.

He nodded as he dried his hands on a paper towel. "I also know that you're into me just as much as I'm into you. My spies have told me about some of the conversations you and your friend Bree have had about me."

My mouth dropped open in shock, and he grinned.

I didn't think I could be any more surprised than I was at the moment, but I realized I was wrong when Allen took my hand and looked deep into my eyes. "Courtland, will you be my girlfriend?"

four

---

sometimes I wake in the middle of the night wondering if I dreamed the night Allen asked me to be his girlfriend, but then I slip one of the letters he's written me from under my pillow and reread it or look at all the text messages he's sent me over the last month and realize that it's very real.

Allen Benson, star basketball player, likes me, and although I haven't told him yet, I love him. Since that first night he came to my house, he's been here every chance he gets, and we get together during lunch and study hall and whenever we have a few free moments. We're the new it couple at school, and I can't believe it.

Momma thinks it's cute what Allen and I have. She says he's a nice guy who comes from a good family. Cory likes him, too. I've never seen my little sister open up to someone as quickly as she's done with Allen. They spend time playing video games and the three of us shoot hoops.

Even Daddy came around. The few times he was home

when Allen was there, they actually held decent conversations. Daddy even came to see Allen play, which surprised me because it had been a while since he came to any activity I participated in.

I guess Daddy was really feeling Allen because a few weeks before my seventeenth birthday, Aunt Dani, who was thrilled I was dating a baller and who had decided to stay in Birmingham indefinitely, stopped by and went off on my parents for not letting me date. Daddy came into the kitchen where Allen and I were studying for finals, which were going to take place the week after Thanksgiving, which was only a few days away.

"You can go out with her," Daddy said, "but Dani has to go with you."

It took a second for his words to register, but when they did, Allen and I looked at each other in surprise.

"Thank you," he said, getting up to shake Daddy's hand.

I walked over and hugged Daddy, trying to ignore the alcohol I smelled on his breath and trying not to think about how awkward it felt. The last time I had really hugged Daddy was at my junior high school graduation. That night had been one of the best of my life. Daddy hadn't stopped grinning the whole time, and as I was getting ready for bed, he came into my room and told me how proud he was of me and how much he loved me. We had really talked that night. He had told me how he felt about finding out right after he finished high school he was adopted and how he always dreamed of becoming a police officer.

His faith in me that night was what made me decide I was going to lose weight, and I vowed I would always pursue my dreams.

"Thank you, Daddy." I looked over his shoulder to where Momma and Aunt Dani were standing, and Aunt Dani winked. I reminded myself to thank her later.

Daddy just kind of grunted.

Allen kissed me on the cheek, then we both walked over and gave Momma a hug.

"Thank you," I said. "I know you had something to do with this."

She grinned at us both. "You're welcome," she said. "I remember what it was like to be young and in love. You guys behave yourselves, and don't make me regret this."

"I promise to take good care of your daughter," Allen vowed.

"So, Allen, why don't you hook me up with one of your fine baller friends?" Aunt Dani said. "Make sure he's older, though, and has plenty of money. At my age, I don't have time to be dating little boys."

Allen grinned. "I know just the guy."

Aunt Dani called me a couple of days later and told me she was going to treat me to a new outfit for my date. Allen and I had decided to go out to dinner then to the homecoming dance, and Momma and Daddy had agreed we could go to the dance without Aunt Dani and her date. I was all for something new to wear, so we headed to the Galleria mall the weekend before homecoming.

"How's my favorite niece?" she asked, and I laughed, knowing that's really how she felt.

My grandparents had three children together, and Aunt Dani was my grandfather's daughter from another relationship. It didn't take a genius to figure out my granddaddy had cheated on my grandma, but for as long as I could remember, Aunt Dani had always been at family events, and although there were several other grandkids, including a few more girls, I was the oldest, and my grandparents and my aunt spoiled me rotten.

"Hey, Aunt Dani," I said, giving her a hug.

"How was the game yesterday?" she asked.

I filled her in, and she promised to come see me before the end of the season.

"You're coming to regionals when we make it, right?" I asked.

"Where's it going to be this year?" she asked.

"It's actually in Birmingham, at the Civic Center," I said.

"It's on like popcorn," she said. "I'll be there, just let me know when."

I cracked up. Every now and then, Aunt Dani would use these outdated phrases, and I just found them funny.

"Aunt Dani, nobody says that anymore," I said.

"Then I'm just going to bring it back," she said.

We laughed and talked all the way to the mall. It felt good to be with my aunt again, just the two of us.

"Do they have Chanel here?" Aunt Dani asked as she pulled into a spot. She put the car in gear then reached into her Coach bag for some lipstick.

"No," Cory said, springing up from the trunk area of Aunt Dani's SUV. Aunt Dani and I both screamed.

"Girl…" Aunt Dani said, clutching her chest.

"Munchkin, what has Momma told you about hiding from people and scaring them?" I said. Cory hadn't done it in a couple years, and Momma said it was just a phase she had been going through, but obviously not, since she was doing it again.

Cory was laughing so hard as she tried to climb over the backseat that she fell on the floor.

"That's not funny," I said. "You're gonna get hurt doing that." I shook my head and looked at the floor. Aunt Dani was still trying to recover. Her eyes were huge like she'd seen a ghost, and the lipstick she'd been putting on when Cory scared us had ended up on her cheek like a bright red jagged scar. "Say you're sorry."

"Sorry," Cory said, but I knew she really didn't mean it.

"What are you doing here, anyway?" I asked.

"I wanted to come, too, and I knew if I asked you'd say no."

I just shook my head, knowing she was right. "Come on," I said before turning to Aunt Dani. "You ready?"

She looked in the mirror. "Do I look ready? I should spank you, Cory, with your bad behind."

Cory looked really hurt.

"She's not bad," I said, jumping to her defense.

Aunt Dani started to say something, but decided to repair her makeup instead. We sat there for about twenty minutes waiting on her, and Cory played her Game Boy while Allen and I texted each other, mainly about our date. Finally he called me.

"Where are you?" he asked.

"At the mall," I said. "Where are you?"

"Just chilling at home. Who are you with?"

"My aunt and sister. Why?"

"I just wanted to make sure ain't nobody hitting on my baby," he said. He got quiet, and I heard loud music then someone talking in the background, but I couldn't hear what the person was saying. "Hey, my mom is calling me," he said after a few seconds.

"I didn't know you were seeing your mom this weekend."

"Yeah," he said. "I'll call you later." He turned up the music, then whispered, "I love you."

"I love you, too," I said. It was the first time I had said the words to him, and it felt good knowing he felt the same way and he had said it first.

"Ain't that sweet?" Aunt Dani said, ruining the moment. "You ready?" She looked at me like she'd been waiting on me.

"Yes, ma'am," I said, and she looked at me like I was crazy.

"I know you didn't just call me ma'am."

"Sorry," I said. Sometimes I forgot she was only a few years older than me. I mean, she had lived in New York and L.A. She had dated celebrities. Sometimes it just seemed like she was older.

Until she stepped out of the car.

Then I thought she was my age, if not younger.

She had on these tight pants with something written on the butt and a too-little T-shirt with BABE across her breasts and some high-heeled sandals, although it was November.

Momma didn't let me wear clothes with writing on it because she said it caused people to stare at body parts they shouldn't be focused on, and I realized she was right because I couldn't help but look at Aunt Dani's butt and breasts.

It was noon before we finally made it into the mall, and it was packed. We found my outfit in the first store we went in, Forever 21, but Aunt Dani insisted on going in almost every store, and she used her American Express in each of them. We stopped at the jewelry counter in Macy's because she said we had to accessorize my outfit, and although I was tired, I agreed.

We parked Cory at one of the makeup counter chairs with all our bags and a new PlayStation Portable, complete with nine or ten games, courtesy of Aunt Dani, then went to look at the jewelry.

Aunt Dani picked out three or four necklaces and showed them to me. "Which one do you like for your outfit?"

"Oh, I don't need a necklace," I said, fingering my purity pearl. "I'm going to wear this."

She looked at my necklace and wrinkled her nose. "You can't wear that ugly thing."

"Why not?" I asked, a little insulted. "This is really special to me."

Her face lit up. "Did Allen give it to you?"

Before I could respond, she said, "I knew I'd rub off on

you. I'm glad to see you're learning how to get things from men while you're still young."

"What?" I asked, confused.

"Girl, now that you've lost all that weight, you can hang with me, and we can pull all types of men. I can hook you up with one who will get you diamonds."

"I don't want you to hook me up with anyone else," I said. "I want to be with Allen. Anyway, he didn't give me this necklace. This is my purity pearl."

She turned up her lip and rolled her eyes at someone who was trying to sidestep her. "It's a what?" she asked.

I explained about Worth the Wait and what the pearl represented, and she laughed so loud people stopped and looked at us. I guess she liked the attention because she started laughing louder and bent over, slapping the glass counter so hard I thought it would crack. She looked at me after she finally caught her breath with tears in her eyes. "Let me guess, your mother made you join?"

I pretended to study some earrings so I didn't have to respond. "Girl, your mother is tripping. I can't believe she made you join a virgin club. Has she told you anything about sex?"

"Yes," I mumbled, not believing we were having this conversation in the mall.

She shook her head. "I don't want to know what she said. Obviously the two of us are going to have to talk so I can school you on the real deal about men. What are you doing tonight?"

"Bree and I are going to Spinners," I said, referring to the skating rink where everyone hung out.

"Well, we'll do it some other time," she said. "So which necklace are you going to get?"

"I'll just wear this one," I said. "Allen likes the necklace and the fact that I'm a virgin, so that's all that matters to me."

"You told him you're a virgin?" she asked.

"Yeah," I said.

"And he liked it?" she said thoughtfully. "Interesting."

The night of the homecoming dance, Allen was still pumped because our team had won the homecoming game, and I was excited because despite my dream the first day of school, we had nailed our halftime show.

I wanted Bree to come over to help me get dressed for my date, but she was out of town with her family, so I asked Candy, the co-captain of the cheerleading squad, to come over since Aunt Dani said she'd meet Allen and me at the restaurant.

"So are you excited?" Candy asked.

"Yes and no," I said as I stood in the mirror combing my hair.

"Why yes and no?" Candy asked curiously.

"Yes because it's my first date, and no because I'm so used to being around Allen that I don't think it will be any different." I looked at my hair and threw the comb down in frustration.

It had grown some more, and I felt as though there was

nothing I could do with it. I was seriously thinking about getting it cut.

Candy eased me into the chair in front of my vanity and picked up the comb.

"So where did you guys decide to go for dinner?" she asked, plugging in a curling iron.

"I have no idea. Allen said he wanted to surprise me," I said.

Candy nodded.

"You really like him, huh?" she said.

I blushed. "Yeah, I do," I admitted. "I still can't believe he likes me. He doesn't even mind my being in Worth the Wait."

"Why would he?" she asked curiously.

I shrugged. "I don't know. Some of the girls who are members say their boyfriends have a problem with them being in a virgin club. Have you ever thought about joining?" I asked, realizing I had never asked her.

She laughed. "I thought about it for a minute, but I decided not to."

"Why not?"

"It just seems to be the in thing right now. I'm secure enough in my virginity not to need a club to back my decision."

I nodded. I hadn't thought about it like that.

We sat in silence while she worked on my hair before we finally made eye contact in the mirror.

"Are you okay?" I asked. She looked like she had something on her mind.

"Sure," she said, tapping my shoulder to let me know she was done. I looked in the mirror, and my hair looked amazing. Candy had parted it differently, and done it in spiral curls that really complemented my face.

"This looks great," I said, getting up to hug her. "Can you help me into my dress?"

Aunt Dani and I had settled on a navy dress and some matching heels. I wore my purity necklace, although Aunt Dani continued to try and talk me out of it. I thought I looked really good—mature but not too old—and Momma agreed when I modeled the outfit for her. Candy seemed to like the outfit, too.

"Well, I guess I'm ready," I said, glancing at the clock. Allen was supposed to arrive at seven, so I still had a few minutes. "Do you think we should add some extra practices next week? I want to make sure we're ready for regionals," I said.

"Sounds good," Candy said, looking distracted.

I touched her shoulder. "Hey, what's going on with you? Are you sure you're okay?"

Candy took a deep breath. "I need to tell you something," she said, "but I don't want you to get mad at me or think I'm trying to ruin your relationship."

"Okay," I said slowly. For some reason the way Candy had acted toward Allen when we saw him near the fountain flashed through my mind. I wondered if she was going to tell me she liked Allen—or worse, they had dated.

"I know someone who used to date Allen," she confessed.

"Girl, is that what's been bothering you?" I said, and

laughed. "Everybody has history. What Allen did before we dated doesn't concern me." I picked up my purse and checked it to make sure I had all my essentials, including my cell phone and my emergency twenty-dollar bill.

"But that's just it, it does concern you—or at least it might," she said.

"Candy, what's going on? Just tell me," I insisted, tired of her beating around the bush.

She grabbed my hand. "Courtland, my friend said that Allen used to hit her."

I couldn't help it. I burst into laughter. "That's your big secret? Girl, please. Allen wouldn't hurt a fly."

"But why would she lie about something like that?" Candy asked.

I stopped laughing, realizing she was serious. "Let me ask you something," I said. "Did Allen break up with her, or did she break up with him?"

"What does that have to do with anything?" Candy asked.

"Just answer the question," I said.

"I think he broke up with her," she admitted.

"Just what I thought," I muttered before looking at her. "Don't you see what's happening?"

"No," Candy said.

"She's angry Allen dumped her, and she's trying to get back at him. She probably heard we were going together and didn't like it, so she told you that stupid mess trying to break us up so she could get back with him."

Candy shook her head. "She's not that type of person, Courtland," she said.

I sighed, trying to hide my frustration. I couldn't believe Candy was trying to ruin the biggest night of my life. "Okay, let's say Allen did beat her. Why did she stay with him? Why didn't she break up with him?"

Candy shrugged. "I really can't answer that," she said. "All I know is what she told me, and I would never forgive myself if I didn't say anything and something happened to you."

I laughed. "Girl, please, the only thing that's going to happen to me is that I'm going to go have some fun with my man."

She gave me a sad smile. "I hope for your sake that's all that happens."

"Is that why you acted so funky with him that night at the fountain?"

"Yes," she admitted.

Candy's vibe was starting to mess up my evening. "Well, since I'm dressed, you can leave. I'm sure you want to get dressed for the dance," I said, hoping I didn't sound as rude as my words felt. She was going with a group of cheerleaders, and they weren't going to leave until later.

"Yeah," she said, catching my hint. She gathered her things and gave me a hug I didn't return. "I really hope you have a good time, Courtland."

Allen arrived at seven sharp, looking good in a navy suit, white shirt and a navy and red tie. It was as though we had planned our outfits so we matched.

"Don't you two look nice," Momma said as I came downstairs after she let Allen in.

She grabbed her digital camera off the coffee table and began snapping pictures while Daddy sat there pretending to read the paper. I noticed he still had on his police uniform, and I wondered if he had to go back to work, but I didn't bother to ask.

"Thank you, Mrs. M.," Allen said. He leaned over and gave me a kiss on the cheek. "You look beautiful, Courtland," he said, handing me a wrist corsage.

"So do you," I said, accepting it.

"You ready?" he asked.

I nodded. As I was going to grab my purse and coat, Daddy stood. "Before you go, I need a DNA sample," he said.

My mouth dropped open, and Allen looked at me, not sure if Daddy was serious. Honestly, I wasn't sure either until Momma said, "Corwin, leave that boy alone."

I burst out laughing, and Momma looked up from the digital camera. "Oh, Lord," she muttered as she started taking pictures.

"Daddy, you're silly," Cory said, and giggled.

"Naw, baby, I'm crazy," Daddy said. "Allen is a nice guy, but I want him to know Courtland's daddy is crazy, and he won't hesitate to act a fool if someone hurts his daughter."

I shook my head and looked at Allen, whose eyes widened as Daddy plopped down in a recliner, grabbed a handful of peppermints from the bowl on the table and started eating them with the wrappers on. After a few seconds he spit them out and grinned.

"I'm just messing with you," he said to Allen, who looked relieved.

Daddy grinned, and I relaxed. Daddy excused himself, and Allen and I stood posing for pictures. I was relieved when Momma said the memory card was full. She started deleting pictures, and I used the break to get out of there.

I gathered my purse, and Momma called for Daddy.

"Corwin, the kids are leaving. Come say goodbye," she said.

I went to the hallway mirror to check my makeup, stopping short when I saw Daddy's reflection over my shoulder. I turned around, not believing what I was seeing.

Daddy looked a hot mess as Momma would say. He had a necktie around his head like a scarf, his shirt was half out of his pants, his belt was wrapped around his leg and he'd somehow managed to put a sock on over his shoe.

When I thought we were free to go, he turned to Allen. "I need to talk to you," he told Allen, and I groaned to myself. I thought we were going to get away without him saying anything more.

"Yes, sir," Allen said.

I gave Momma a look, and she shrugged. She had already given me the talk about behaving myself like a Christian young lady, spending an hour talking about why abstinence was the only sure way of not getting pregnant or getting an STD. I had tuned most of it out. The girls in Worth the Wait had already told me she'd do that.

It wasn't that I hadn't thought about having sex with Allen because I had, but I knew it wasn't something I was ready to do anytime soon. I was really serious about the vow I had taken to stay a virgin until I got married, and Allen was cool with it.

Daddy and Allen stayed gone for about ten minutes. When they came back, Allen winked at me, letting me know everything was okay, then he helped me into my coat.

"You guys have a good time," Momma called, while Daddy stood next to her with his hand resting on his gun. "Allen, have my baby back here by eleven."

I turned and looked at Momma. We hadn't discussed my curfew, but I had assumed it wouldn't be so early. I mean, granted she had given me a little leeway since I had to be home by ten-thirty when I hung with my friends and Aunt Dani would be there for part of the night, but I figured she would at least let me stay out until midnight since it was homecoming and my first date.

I thought about saying something, but Allen took my hand and squeezed, telling me to let it go. "Not a problem, ma'am."

"Courtland, do you have that stuff I gave you?" Momma asked. It took me a second to realize she meant the twenty dollars, and I nodded.

"Good," she said, kissing me. "Y'all be careful and have a good time."

Momma and Daddy stood in the doorway until we pulled away in Allen's father's Mercedes.

"Where's your car?" I asked, looking around as though

his Ford Explorer would appear. He had gotten it shortly after he had started coming to visit me when his other car broke down, but I had yet to ride in it since Momma wouldn't let Allen drive me home from school. Hopefully all of that was about to change now that we were on our official first date.

"I figured we needed something a little more special for this occasion," he said. "You don't like this car?"

"Man, are you crazy? It's beautiful," I said. "Thank you for making this night special for me. If I forget to tell you, I had a wonderful time tonight." I had heard Julia Roberts say that in the old movie *Pretty Woman,* and I decided to claim it as my own.

"Anything for my baby," he said, and I smiled.

"So where are we going?"

"Don't you want to be surprised?"

"Not really," I said, although I loved surprises. "I've been trying to think of where it could be since Daddy said we could go out." I looked at Allen and grinned. "We're on our first date. Can you believe it?"

He smiled, and his dimple, appeared. "I've been dreaming about this day for months," he said.

"Really?" I said. "That is so sweet."

"No, you're so sweet." He grabbed my hand and kissed it, then we held hands all the way to the restaurant.

When we arrived at the Empire Club, my mouth fell open. "Are you kidding me?" I asked. The restaurant was one of the most expensive in Birmingham. Momma had told me one time that they printed the menus without prices, and that if you had to ask how much something was, you couldn't afford to eat there.

Allen laughed. "You know I had to make sure I did this thing right. Come on." He grabbed my hand after he gave the valet the keys, and we headed inside.

There was a man who looked vaguely familiar standing at the front entrance. Allen walked over and shook his hand, then waved me over and introduced me.

"Courtland, this is Miles King, the head coach for the Atlanta Sentinels."

"Nice to meet you," I said, shaking his hand. "I knew you looked familiar. I've seen you on ESPN a few times." I didn't add that Allen had told me he was interested in signing with the Sentinels. I vaguely remembered hearing players weren't supposed to deal with coaches when they were being recruited. I looked at Allen with a question in my eyes, but he just smiled.

"So what are you doing here?" Allen asked.

"Randy's mom was rushed to the hospital, so he asked me to come here tonight in his place."

"Who's Randy?" I asked.

"He's a trainer I met this summer during camp," Allen explained. "I didn't know you guys knew each other."

"He's my frat brother," Miles said. "I hope it's okay that I came. I don't want to get you in any trouble. I can assure you that I'm not planning on talking about basketball at all tonight. I can't wait to see the young lady you have to introduce to me."

I breathed a sigh of relief that Allen hadn't known

about Miles coming, then studied Miles. He actually was a nice-looking guy. He looked like he was my parents' age, in his late thirties or early forties, and he sported a low fade and a mustache. I figured Aunt Dani would like him.

"Where's your aunt?" Allen asked me, checking his watch. "Our reservation is for seven-thirty."

As though she was waiting for someone to mention her, Aunt Dani breezed through the door.

"Hey, Corky," she said, switching her way over to me in these ridiculously high heels.

I groaned to myself, but I wasn't sure if it was because she used my nickname or because of what she had on. Her shoes were red patent leather, and she had on black fishnets and a red strapless dress that barely covered her butt. She also had on a mink stole and her freshly done weave was blond. She reminded me of Hottie from *Flavor of Love Girls: Charm School.*

She didn't wait for me to respond before turning to Miles. "Miles King, is that you?"

"You guys know each other?" I asked.

She laughed. "Girl, please. You know I know all the major players in the big cities." She turned to Miles. "I don't need an introduction, but I'm Loretta Danielle Dennis. You can call me Loretta. All my friends do."

I had to try hard to keep from laughing, since I didn't know anyone who called her Loretta.

Miles smiled. Before we could say anything, the maître d' walked up and told us to follow him.

Once we were seated, I looked around, impressed by

the ambience. "Is this your first time here?" I asked Allen, picking up a menu. Momma was right. There weren't any prices on it.

He shook his head. "Nah. My dad has brought me here a couple of times."

"So what do you recommend?"

Allen made a few suggestions, and I finally settled on shrimp cocktail to start followed by filet mignon with a baked potato and salad. Allen and Miles ordered crab cakes and shrimp scampi, and Aunt Dani ordered two appetizers followed by a surf and turf, which I learned was a combination of lobster and steak, along with a bottle of Cristal champagne, which I knew had to be expensive because all the celebrities had it in their refrigerators on old episodes of *Cribs*. I thought it was rude to order so much, but the guys didn't seem to mind.

"Is my food too expensive?" I asked Allen, thinking maybe I had overdone it.

"Girl, quit tripping. Get what you want. Money's no object when it comes to you."

"You're so sweet," I said.

"You know I love you, right?" he leaned over and whispered.

My heart stopped. He had only said it once before, and I had relived that moment over and over in my mind, wondering if it had been a dream. This was the first time he was saying the words to my face.

"I love you, too," I said. "More than you know."

"Ahh, isn't that sweet? Y'all need to get a room," Aunt

Dani said, messing up the moment again. She started laughing all loud. "I forgot my niece doesn't need a room." She leaned over to Miles and said loud enough for the entire restaurant to hear, "She's a virgin."

My face turned bright red, if that was possible. I stared at my plate, wishing I could crawl under it.

Allen squeezed my hand, but it didn't really help. "I think it's cool that Courtland's a virgin," he said. "I've been thinking about joining her club, too."

I looked up in surprise, and he winked at me.

"Boy, please. You're about to go pro. In a few months you'll have so many women throwing themselves at you, you won't be able to see straight. They're probably already throwing themselves at you."

"Just because they throw it doesn't mean I have to catch it," he said. "Courtland is the only woman I want to be with."

Allen and I grinned at each other and we all made small talk until the waiter brought our salads. Allen fed me a bite of his Caesar salad, which was amazing.

The waiter smiled at us when he came to refill our water glasses. "It's so nice to see young people in love," he said.

I smiled. It felt good to be in love.

"It sure is," Aunt Dani said. She was already on her third glass of Cristal, and she was still talking loud. "You know what, Miles? Let's get our own table and give these kids some privacy. They're going to be leaving soon for the homecoming dance, if they actually go," Aunt Dani said, giving us a sly wink, trying to look sexy.

I was glad she made the suggestion, and I relaxed a little when Allen and I were finally alone.

"So what stuff was your mother asking you if you had?" Allen asked as we continued to eat.

"Oh," I said, laughing, "she gave me twenty dollars, which she insisted I keep with me at all times in case you trip."

He got this strange expression. "Why would she think I would trip on you?" he asked.

"I don't think she meant you, really," I explained. "I think she just meant guys in general."

"Why would she feel that way?"

I shrugged. "Maybe some guy tripped on her when she was growing up. Who knows? You know we don't get half the stuff our parents tell us to do."

Allen wiped his mouth and threw his napkin on his plate. Before it had landed, a waiter came and refolded it so it looked like a bird, then he used some metal thing to scrape up the crumbs that had fallen on the table.

"Man, both of your parents are tripping. Do you know your dad threatened me while we were in the kitchen?"

"Are you serious?" I asked, my eyes getting big. "What did he say?"

Allen moved aside as the waiter slid our appetizers in front of us before he continued. "Something about you being his baby, and if I laid a hand on you he'd shoot first and ask questions later."

I laughed under my breath, unable to imagine my daddy saying something like that. I thought about sharing my thoughts with Allen, but instead I said, "You know my parents can be overprotective. I'm their baby girl."

"You're my baby girl, too," he said, grasping my hand so tight my fingers started hurting. I looked down at our clasped hands, and Allen must have realized how hard he was squeezing because he let go. "Courtland, you know I'd never do anything to hurt you, right? You're the only woman I've ever loved."

The image of the hickey he had on his neck flashed through my mind, but I brushed it away. "You're the only man I've ever loved," I said. "I'd never hurt you, either."

Allen smiled before he fed me some of his crab cake. I returned the favor by giving him some of my shrimp, and we both agreed mine was better. We ended up sharing it, which was fine with me.

The food arrived a few minutes later. While we were eating, a band started playing and couples began to get up and dance. The music was slow and beautiful and so infectious that before I knew it, I was moving in my seat.

"I guess you want to dance," Allen joked.

"I don't, but my body does," I said.

"What else does your body want?" he said, giving me a kiss that almost landed on my lips.

I looked down at my plate and tried not to blush. We had talked about sex before, and although Allen had admitted he wasn't a virgin, he promised me there was no pressure for me to sleep with him.

"Okay, I'm not going to tease you," he said. He held

out his hand, and I shyly took it so he could escort me to the dance floor.

I didn't expect Allen to be as graceful as he was. He wrapped his arms around me, and I felt so protected and loved.

We danced through two songs until Aunt Dani pulled Miles on the floor, backing that thang up like she was in the club. Allen thought it was funny, but it killed my mood. We headed back to the table to finish our food. The waiter was nice enough to warm it up for us, and it tasted even better than it had originally, if that was possible.

After we ordered dessert, I glanced at my watch. "I can't believe it's only eight-thirty," I said. "We have time to stop by the homecoming dance and hang out for a while. What are you going to do with me for the rest of the evening?" I realized how my question sounded and shook my head. "That didn't come out the right way."

"It's okay," Allen said. "I know what you meant. Do you want to skip the dance? I have a few more surprises up my sleeve."

I seriously thought about what he was saying. Although I wanted to go to the dance to show off my man, more than that, I wanted to spend some time alone with Allen, which we had never really done, since we were always around others at school or my house.

"We don't have to go to the dance if you don't want to. Are you going to tell me where we're going?" I asked.

"You'll see," he said mysteriously.

I almost didn't finish my dessert I was so excited about where Allen was going to take me.

I watched as Allen paid the bill, and I couldn't believe it when he put down three crisp hundred-dollar bills into the holder with the receipt.

"Was our food really that much?" I asked in amazement. "I'm sorry. I didn't realize it was that expensive here."

"It's not a problem," he said. "I paid for your aunt and Miles, too."

"Are you sure?" I asked, looking doubtful.

"Baby, it's fine," he assured me.

"How can you afford this?" I asked.

He laughed.

"Seriously, I'm not trying to be funny or get all in your business, but I know you don't work 'cause you're too busy practicing."

"I'm not trying to keep any secrets from you, so don't worry about getting in my business—my business is your business," he said. "My dad makes pretty decent money as an engineer, and I get an allowance, so some of that money is what I've saved. Between practice, school and church, I don't normally go out much, but I have a feeling that's about to change," he said, smiling at me. "Besides that, every now and then some of the recruiters hit me off."

"But isn't that illegal?" I asked.

"I won't tell if you won't."

"Did Miles give you that money?" I asked, suddenly worried.

Allen laughed. "Miles is too straight for him to do anything outside of NBA recruiting regulations. I've only met him one other time, but he's not one of the coaches who would bend the rules. I'm surprised he came tonight. He must be hard up for a woman."

I decided that if Allen wasn't bothered by what he was doing, I wasn't going to be, either, but his words really bothered me. I knew what he was doing wasn't right, and I couldn't help but say something.

"Please don't take any more money from the recruiters," I said after the waiter took our money.

Allen looked at me like I was crazy. "Why not?" he said. "How else am I going to do nice things for you?"

Immediately I felt guilty. Although deep down I knew I hadn't done anything wrong, I believed that the only reason Allen had accepted the money was because he felt like he had to to keep me.

I grabbed his hand and looked him in the eye. "Allen, you don't have to take me to fancy restaurants," I said. "We can go to McDonald's or even sit at home on my sofa, and I'd be happy. I just enjoy spending time with you."

"But I wouldn't be happy," he said. "How does it look, me going pro and my girl is sitting up in McDonald's. That's not going to happen."

"But, baby—"

"It's not happening, Courtland," he said, cutting me off. "You deserve the best, and I'm going to do whatever I need to to make sure you get it."

I opened my mouth to say something else.

"End of discussion," he said.

I just nodded as I gathered my purse. We met Aunt Dani and Miles at the entrance, and Aunt Dani was barely able to stand she was so drunk. I was going to take her home, but Miles said he didn't want to ruin our date and he'd make sure she got there safely. It took a while for me to agree. I mean, Miles seemed cool and all, but for all I knew, he could be a serial killer.

After the valet brought the car around and Allen helped me in, he pulled out of the parking lot, then drove to Griffith Park. I looked up in surprise.

"Did we just have our first argument in the restaurant?" he asked.

I smiled. "I guess so," I said.

"I'm sorry. I didn't mean to upset you. I wanted this to be a perfect night for you."

"It has been," I said. "It's just that…"

"What?" he asked. Before I could respond, he got out of the car and came around to help me out, then he led me to the swings on the playground, seated me in one and began pushing me. "It's just what?"

"This isn't about money for me. I know a lot of girls might be after you because of the money they think you're going to make when you go pro, but I love you, Allen. You could be broke, and I would still love you."

"And that's exactly why I'm with you. I've dated other girls before, and you might not be the prettiest one, but I've known for a while that you've had my back. I need someone like you in my life."

I was a bit insulted by his comment about me not being the prettiest, but I tried not to let it show. Instead I focused on what he had said about needing me in his life. "I need you, too," I said.

He came and stood in front of me, stopping the swing, then he leaned down and kissed me so hard I couldn't breathe. I had never been kissed like that before in my life. It was so incredible. When he eased his tongue into my mouth, I didn't protest. Instead, I welcomed it, and I returned the favor, getting so caught up in the kiss and this man. I still couldn't believe that Allen Benson was my boyfriend.

It wasn't until I felt Allen's hands on my butt that reality set in. As much as I didn't want to, I backed away.

"What's the matter?" he asked, his voice low and deep. "I know you want me. This would be a great way to end our first date."

"We've got to stop," I said.

He pulled me back to him and kissed me gently. "It's okay. Nobody has to know."

I didn't want to admit that I wanted to do more than kiss him right then. I glanced at my watch and realized it was after nine. "We need to get going. I have to be home soon," I said, not knowing what else to say.

Allen sat down in the swing and pulled me onto his lap. "We still have some time," he whispered, giving my neck a feather-soft kiss. It felt so good. Before I knew it, I had turned so I was facing him, and we were kissing again. Allen rubbed his hands up and down my back, pulling me close, and I ran my fingers over his hair and his muscular shoulders.

I had never felt anything like what was going on inside my body, and although I kept telling myself we needed to stop, my lips and tongue seemed to have a mind of their own.

It wasn't until a bright light shone in our faces that I pulled away.

"Courtland?" someone asked.

I squinted against the light, using my hand to shield my eyes.

"Yes," I said. It took me only a second to take in the officer's uniform. The officer focused the light on the ground, and I realized it was my daddy's old partner, William Henderson.

I jumped out of Allen's lap so fast I almost fell on the ground. "Hey, Officer Henderson," I said. "We were just…uh…talking."

He laughed. "Really?" he asked, arching his eyebrow. He turned to look at Allen, who stood and held out his hand.

"Allen Benson," he said, turning on the charm. "I was just about to take Courtland home."

"I think that's a good idea," Officer Henderson said before turning to me. "How's your father?"

"He's okay," I said, smoothing my hair. I knew I had to be looking crazy.

"Tell him I said hello, and don't let me catch you two out here again," he said, which I took as a warning that he would tell Daddy if he did.

"Yes, sir," Allen said, reaching out to shake his hand again. "I can assure you it won't happen again. Thank you, sir."

Officer Henderson watched us as we got in the car and drove away.

"Do you think he's going to tell my daddy?" I asked, pulling down the visor so I could fix my hair.

"So what if he does? We weren't doing anything but kissing," Allen said.

I smacked my lips. "After the conversation you had with my daddy earlier, you want him to find out we were kissing?" I thought about saying that it was more than that, but I decided not to bring it up.

"Good point," Allen said.

"You know what, my momma is going to want to know all about the dance, since this was my first date. What am I supposed to tell her? Maybe we should at least stop through there."

Allen frowned. "I hadn't thought about that. Why don't you call one of your girls and get the details?"

I reluctantly called Candy and she gave me a rundown of what we'd missed. After promising to call her the next morning, I gave Allen the information, and we coordinated our stories, so if Momma asked any questions we wouldn't contradict each other.

We sat in silence for a few minutes. "Girl, where'd you learn how to kiss like that? I thought you told me you've never had a boyfriend," Allen finally said.

"I don't know," I said. "I did what came natural. You were a good teacher."

Allen lifted one side of his mouth in a smile. "So you're sure you haven't been with anybody else?"

I tapped him on the arm. "Boy, I told you no. You know how strict my parents are. When would I have the chance?"

"A woman will find the time to do what she wants to do," he said.

I looked at him not believing the words that had just come out of his mouth. "So what are you trying to accuse me of?" I asked, rolling my neck.

I guess Allen realized how he sounded, because he caressed my hair while we were at a stoplight. "I'm sorry. I know you're a virgin," he said, touching my purity necklace. "I just can't stand the thought of you being with another guy."

"And you think I like the thought of you being with another girl?" I said, still a little angry. "We both know I'm not the first girl you've kissed. As a matter of fact, that day you missed our study session, you rolled up with a hickey on your neck, talking about how Coach Patterson wanted to meet with you. Please."

Allen sat back in his seat and stared at me so long I started to feel uncomfortable. He didn't move until the car behind him blew its horn because the light had turned green. He didn't say a word until we pulled up in front of my house where the front porch light was shining bright, welcoming me home.

I reached down to get my purse, and Allen grabbed my wrist, stopping me. "Don't you ever question me about who I see and what I do. Do you hear me?" he asked between clenched teeth.

I tried to pry his hand off me, but his grip only grew

tighter, and the fabric on my sleeve bunched up around my wrist. "Ow, you're hurting me," I said.

"Do you hear me?" he repeated, ignoring my plea. There was this strange look in his eyes and it scared me. I told myself to stay calm, but apparently my heart wasn't listening, because it was running a marathon in my chest.

"Yeah, I hear you," I said, willing to say anything so he would let go of me. When he didn't move, I looked him dead in the eye. "I said I heard you," I repeated, jerking my arm. "Let go of me."

Allen seemed satisfied with my words, because he let go. I wanted to rub my left wrist, which was throbbing, but I decided to wait until I got in the house. I grabbed my purse with my right hand and moved to open the door.

"I've got it," Allen said, getting out of the car before I could protest.

I gave him a tight smile as he helped me out of the car and led me up the stairs. I removed my key from my purse, ignoring Allen, who stood patiently waiting for me to unlock the front door.

"You okay?" Allen asked, pushing my hair out of my eyes. All I could do was nod.

"Did you have a good time?"

I didn't know what to say. I realized that despite Aunt Dani's antics, it had been the perfect evening until the drive home. I was ready to escape to my room, so I just nodded.

"Can I have a kiss?" he said. He pointed to a spot on his cheek, indicating I should kiss him there. I leaned in to do as he had asked, but just as my lips were about to touch his cheek, he turned his head, and our mouths touched.

"I love you, Courtland," he whispered as I let myself in.

I was headed up the stairs when Daddy's voice stopped me. "How'd it go?" he asked from the den.

I stuck my head in and nodded at him.

"William called and told me he saw you," he said, giving me this weird look.

I wasn't sure what Officer Henderson had told Daddy. Finally I said, "Yeah, he told me to tell you hello."

When Daddy didn't say anything else, I turned to leave. "Good night," I said, my back to him.

"Courtland," my daddy called, and I turned around. "Allen's a good guy. I like him. Don't let him get away."

I just nodded.

Momma's bedroom door was cracked open when I walked by, and I saw she had fallen asleep studying her Sunday-school lesson. I thought about turning off her bedside light, but I didn't want to wake her because I knew she'd want to talk. Instead I headed to my room where I took off my coat and got undressed.

I looked at the spot where Allen had grabbed me. Although there wasn't a bruise, it hurt. That's when the tears came. I replayed the evening in my head, trying to figure out what had gone so horribly wrong. What had I done to make Allen so angry with me? He had mentioned me not seeing other guys, so why was it so wrong for me to say something about him not seeing other girls? Was that enough to make him so angry he would put his hands on me?

As I got in bed and cried myself to sleep that night, I realized the day I had been dreaming of all my life had finally come, and it was nothing like my dreams.

I also knew that as much as I loved Allen, I could never see him again.

five

I really didn't feel like going to church the next morning, but Momma wasn't hearing it.

I guess I was pretty quiet because on the drive to church Momma glanced over at me. "You okay?" she asked.

"Yes, ma'am," I said. I pulled out my Bible and pretended to read, hoping she wouldn't ask any more questions.

"So how was your date last night?" she asked. "I thought you would have woken me up when you came in to tell me all the details."

"It was fine," I said and told her about the Empire Club, although I left out the incident at the park and on the drive home.

"That sounds nice," she said. "So when are you guys going out again?"

"I don't know," I said as we pulled up at church. "I'm going to be pretty busy with regionals coming up this weekend."

She nodded but didn't say anything. I jumped out of the

car to end the conversation. I walked Cory over to children's church, and I had just gotten into the church and was about to settle into my favorite back pew when Momma grabbed my left hand.

"You're going to sing today," she said.

"Momma," I whined, "I didn't even come to practice yesterday."

"That's okay. You know all the songs we're singing."

I started to say something, but she gave me the eye, so I headed to the back.

It felt like the entire congregation was watching me during devotion. I couldn't concentrate because I was so busy thinking about my date. I guess I was fidgeting a lot once service started because Momma finally passed me a note telling me to go in the back to the fellowship hall.

I scooted past a few choir members, and she met me back there.

"What is wrong with you?" she demanded.

"I'm tired," I said.

"You weren't too tired to go out last night."

One of the choir members stuck her head in the room. "Sister Murphy, turn off your microphone," she said. "The entire congregation can hear you."

Momma and I looked at each other, embarrassed. I guess she was supposed to sing lead for a song, since that was the only time she wore one of the mikes our church had recently purchased.

I took a sip of water, trying to get myself together. I

whispered a prayer that God would help me. Momma and I headed back to the choir stand, and I tried to focus, but I couldn't get my mind off Allen.

When the musician began playing, I started singing before everyone else, and my off-key voice rang loudly through the church. I looked at the floor, embarrassed, and only pretended to sing the rest of the song as I stared at the clock on the back wall so I wouldn't have to look at anyone in the pews.

I had to endure one more song, the one where Momma sang solo, before I finally sat down.

The church secretary got up to read the announcements, and I tried to figure out a way to sneak my cell phone out of my purse without Momma seeing me so I could check to see if Allen had texted me.

I had just opened my purse when I heard the name *Allen Benson*. I looked up to see Allen looking too fine in a black pinstriped suit, white shirt and a peach tie.

I glanced at Momma, silently asking her if she knew Allen was planning on coming. She quickly shook her head, which meant she didn't know.

After the other visitors were called, they were asked if they had anything to say. All of the other visitors sat down except for Allen.

"First giving honor to God, I just wanted to say good morning and to thank my girlfriend, Courtland Murphy, for inviting me. I will be back again."

People in the congregation were looking at me and a couple of the choir members patted me on the shoulder.

Our pastor, Reverend Russell, walked over to the pulpit. "Welcome, welcome," he greeted. "Thank you for joining us today." He looked over the crowd, and although his back was to me, I could have sworn his eyes landed on Allen.

"Stand up, son," he said. "You're the star player at Grover who they say is going pro, right?"

"Yes, sir," Allen said.

"Well, amen," Pastor Russell said enthusiastically before turning to me. "Courtland has got her a basketball-playing man. Go head, girl."

The congregation laughed and applauded.

Allen caught my eye a few times during service and smiled at me. Before I could stop myself, I smiled back. I couldn't believe he had actually come to my church to see me and had told everyone I was his girlfriend.

During service, I tried to pay attention to the sermon, but my mind kept drifting to the night before. I realized that Allen hadn't meant to hurt me. He probably didn't even realize how strong he was, and it was obvious he was sorry, because he had come to my church.

It was as though he was reading my mind when he walked over to me after service. He gave me a hug and immediately said he was sorry.

I hugged him back and accepted his apology as Momma walked up.

"Is it okay if I take Courtland out to lunch and drive her home, Mrs. M.?" he asked after giving her a hug.

Momma smiled. "It's good to see you, Allen. We

normally go to my parents' house, but I guess it would be okay if she went with you."

We said our goodbyes and walked to Allen's Explorer. On the front seat was a big teddy bear holding a heart that read "I Love You."

I gasped. "That is so sweet," I said as he helped me in. "Thank you."

"Baby, I am so sorry about the way I treated you last night," he said.

Seeing him cry made me cry, too. "It's okay," I said. "I know you didn't mean it."

"Courtland, I would never hurt you," he said. "Please forgive me. I promise you it won't ever happen again."

I listened as he was talking, and I remembered my aunt Dani telling me men always did crazy things because they loved you. She said since Allen was famous, he was under a lot of pressure, and I had to be extra understanding, especially if he put his hands on me or called me out of my name. She said as long as he apologized and bought me a nice gift, I should be cool with whatever he did. Part of me didn't believe her, but then another part of me thought she might be right, since she had dated a lot of men.

Once Allen was finished, I shook my head. "I know you're sorry, but I think we should take a break from each other," I said.

He broke down and cried so hard tears were dripping off his chin. "Please don't do this," he said. "I love you, Courtland. Let me make this right."

His words really were touching me. I wanted to believe

him, I really did, but I was scared to. He lifted my wrist again and started kissing it. "I will never hurt you again, Courtland. I know I shouldn't have gotten so mad last night, but when you accused me of seeing someone else, I was just so hurt...." He took a deep breath. "Please let me show you I can be the man you need."

I realized what he said was true. If I hadn't brought up that whole hickey incident, none of this would have happened. I was as much to blame as he was. He kissed me on the lips, and I crumbled.

"You have to promise you'll never put your hands on me again," I said.

He quickly nodded. "I promise. If I do, you can leave," he said.

"Okay," I agreed, and just like that, we were back together.

I was really looking forward to the Worth the Wait meeting after school that week. I had a lot of questions running through my mind, and I needed some advice from people who I didn't think would judge me.

I had convinced Bree to come to a couple of meetings with me, and she liked them so much that she had joined, too. We were just getting settled when I looked toward the door and frowned.

"What's she doing here?" I whispered to Bree, who glanced at the door without being obvious.

"Andrea said she wanted us to invite people of different races," she reminded me.

"I thought she meant Hispanics and stuff," I said. A girl named Jennifer Perez had recently joined, and she was cool, but I didn't know how I felt about a white girl joining, especially this white girl.

Emily Arrington was on our rival cheerleading team. Although we obviously had a few things in common, I didn't like the fact that I would now have to share Worth the Wait with her.

"What are you doing here?" she came up to me and asked.

"I need to be asking you that," I said, rolling my eyes at her.

She tossed her hair and took a seat in the chair right next to me. "I heard about this club, and I thought I would come check it out. Do you have a problem with that?"

I didn't bother to answer.

"Well, I see we have someone new today," our adviser, Andrea, said. She walked over and gave Emily a hug. "Welcome."

"Thanks," Emily said, giving her biggest cheerleader smile.

I gave her a half smile and rolled my eyes again, knowing she was being fake.

"You guys ready to get started?" Andrea asked.

We all got settled, then after prayer and Bible study, we got right into our discussion. I thought about not bringing up my question because Emily was there, but I really wanted to know.

"If you really love someone and plan to marry them

anyway, do you have to wait until you get married to sleep with them?" I asked.

"Of course you do. You made a pledge, girl," someone said.

"If you're in love with each other and plan to get married anyway, then I say do it," Bree said, and I looked at her in surprise.

"What about the vow we took?" I asked.

"I say you need to keep your vow," Jennifer said. "You're breaking a promise to yourself. Doesn't that mean anything to you?"

"Of course it does," I said. "Let me ask you—do you have a boyfriend?"

"No," Jennifer said defensively. "Why?"

"Because it's easy to say what you won't do when you don't have that temptation staring you in the face," Emily said, and as much as I didn't want to, I found myself agreeing with her.

"So what are some ways you can avoid temptation?" Andrea asked.

We all grew quiet as we sat deep in thought.

"You can avoid being alone with guys," someone said.

"Is that realistic?" someone else asked.

"For me it is," Jennifer said. She turned to me. "I had a boyfriend, but we broke up because I wouldn't have sex with him. He came with that old tired line, 'If you really loved me...' I was like, 'Boy, please, if you love me, you'll wait.' He broke up with me the next week, and I'm not going to lie and say it didn't hurt, but then I thought about how I would have been feeling if I had slept with him and then he would have broken up with me."

I hadn't thought about it like that, but what Jennifer said made sense. Until Allen put a ring on my finger and actually became my husband, there was no guarantee he would marry me, so what was to stop him from walking away if I gave in? Still, that didn't change the fact that I was feeling some serious things that I had never had to deal with before.

I had tried talking with Aunt Dani about my feelings, and she had encouraged me to act on them, but deep down, I didn't feel like that was the right thing to do.

"I say there's nothing wrong with sleeping with someone if the two of you really love each other," Emily said.

A few of us looked at her like she was crazy.

"If you feel that way, why are you here?" Jennifer asked.

"Because guys find virgins sexy," Emily said. "They all want to think they'll be the ones to make you change your mind. If the right guy comes along, I'm down. If I really loved him, I wouldn't mind having his baby before we got married, too. That way, I would have a part of him with me forever."

I couldn't believe what I was hearing. I sat waiting for Andrea to tell Emily she had to leave, since she seemed to have joined the group for all the wrong reasons, but she didn't. Instead she said, "I'm sorry you feel that way, Emily. I really hope you'll change your mind after you've been with us for a while."

Emily just shrugged and pulled out her phone to send a text message to someone.

We continued our discussion for the next hour, but by the time we were done, I still didn't have any clear answers about whether I should move my relationship with Allen to the next level. He said he loved me, and I loved him, but was that enough to make me break my pledge?

SIX

Allen was true to his word. He went out of his way to be a great boyfriend. When we competed during regionals, he was sitting right there with Momma, Cory, Aunt Dani and the members of Worth the Wait, cheering me on. He even ran out onto the mat when we took first place and swung me around.

Daddy muttered something about public displays of affection when he saw that little scene played out on the news, but that was his problem.

Basketball season was in full swing, so Allen and I really only saw each other during school and sometimes Saturday nights or Sunday afternoons if he didn't have to play. He came to my church a couple of times, and the members started to joke that he should join.

He even let me meet his father, after I asked, then afterward we stopped by his mom and stepdad's house. They were actually very cool. They spoiled Allen rotten since he was the only child. I thought his mother might try and act funny with me since I had heard that women can be protective of their only sons, but she acted like she really liked me.

Allen's mom and stepdad seemed to really enjoy being together. All through dinner they held hands and joked with each other. I had never seen anything like it in my life. My parents couldn't spend ten minutes in the same room without tension.

On the drive home, I was kind of quiet. Allen finally glanced at me and said, "Are you okay?"

I smiled at him. "Yeah, I'm cool," I said. "I was just thinking about your mom and stepdad. Are they always that affectionate?"

Allen shrugged. "I guess. If you ask me, they're too old for that."

I laughed. "I think it's sweet. How long have they been married?"

"About twelve years. They were high school sweethearts, but they broke up for a couple of years during college and my mom married my dad. After my parents divorced, she ran into my stepdad and they realized they couldn't live without each other, so they got married," he said. "What about your parents? How long have they been married?"

"Actually they never did get married," I admitted. I rarely told anyone that since most people just assumed they were.

"Why not?" Allen asked, looking at me in surprise.

"Momma said Daddy doesn't believe in marriage. They've been living together since before I was born, so Momma said in the eyes of the law they are married."

"But she wears a wedding band," Allen said.

"Because she's really committed to my dad," I said, shrugging. It occurred to me for the first time that my dad didn't wear a ring, so did that mean he wasn't committed to Momma?

"How do you feel about them not being married?" he asked.

I thought about his question. "Most of the time it doesn't bother me. I feel bad for Momma though. When we talk about when I get married one day, there's this look in her eyes, like she really wishes she could experience that."

"Well, when we get married, we'll make sure to include her in the planning," he said, taking his hand off the steering wheel to hold mine.

I tried not to grin, but I couldn't help it. "You want to marry me?" I asked.

Allen didn't speak until we came to a traffic light, then he turned to look at me. "Of course I do," he said. He stared deep into my eyes. "Courtland, do you know how much I love you? I still can't believe that you love me, too," he said in wonder. "I want to spend my life with you."

The light changed, and Allen continued driving. When he pulled up at my house, he shut off the engine and looked at me.

"I want to spend my life with you, too," I admitted, then hesitated.

"What?" he asked, grabbing my hand.

"It's just that this time next year you'll be playing for

the NBA, and who knows where you'll be. I still have another year of high school—"

"Girl, don't worry. By then, I'll be making so much money I'll be able to fly you to come see me every weekend."

"You'd do that?"

"No doubt," he said, nodding. "I want you wherever I am. You haven't realized that yet?" He leaned over to kiss me, and everything else seemed to disappear. "I love you, Courtland," he whispered when we broke apart.

"I love you, Allen," I said.

seven

MY focus was totally off at cheerleading practice a few days later, and as I was doing a backflip, I landed awkwardly and ended up spraining my ankle. The doctor made me use crutches and miss practice for a couple of weeks, which was not cool at all because we were training for the national competition in Orlando in January.

After a few days, my ankle started feeling better, so I went back to practice. Although my coach refused to let me do any stunts, I did work on my hand movements and making sure our routine was on point.

Candy had offered to drop me off after practice, but I had told her no. Every since she told me that stuff about Allen and his ex, I had become kind of distant. How could I really be cool with a girl who was hating on my man?

I had just changed for practice one afternoon and was trying to decide if I had time to toss a few baskets when a voice stopped me.

"Dang, girl, you looking good these days," he said. "What happened to that fat little girl I went to elementary school with?"

I turned around, already knowing it was Nathaniel Dixon. We had known each other since kindergarten.

"What's going on?" I said, going to give him a hug.

"Apparently you," he said. He looked me up and down, taking in my sports bra and biking shorts, which showed off my shape and my six-pack.

"You are so silly," I said, shoving him and laughing. Nathaniel really was a cutie. When we were in elementary school, I had a serious crush on him, but he never seemed to be interested. "So what have you been up to? I hardly ever see you." I smiled and nodded at a couple of Allen's teammates who were walking past before I refocused on Nathaniel.

"Yeah, I got a job after school, so that's been keeping me busy."

I nodded and glanced up at the clock on the wall. Practice wasn't scheduled to begin for about ten minutes. "Where are you working?"

"At the Publix in Homewood," he said. "They have me bagging groceries, but the money is good, so that's cool."

We stood in silence for a few seconds before he looked at me. "I have a favor to ask," he said.

"What's up?" I asked.

"I'm not doing too well in math this semester, and I need your help. Can we get together during study hall?"

"I can't," I said. "I tutor my boyfriend then."

Nathaniel nodded. "So what's up with you and Mr. NBA? I hear things are pretty heavy between you."

"We're good," I said, smiling.

"He's treating you right?"

I looked at him and laughed. "Do you have to ask?" I said as the image of Allen grabbing me entered my mind. As always when it did, I pushed it away.

"Cool," Nathaniel said. "I just wanted to make sure. Do you think we can get together on Sunday afternoons, then? I would say after school, but like I said, I got this job, and I don't have the time."

I thought about all I had going on. Between school, cheerleading, helping Bree with dance class, Allen and Worth the Wait, I didn't have a lot of free time, but I really wanted to help my friend. "Okay," I said.

Nathaniel nodded. "That's cool. My parents won't let me work on Sundays, anyway. Is your home number still the same?"

"Yeah, but let me give you my cell number." I realized I didn't have anything to write it on, but Nathaniel had his phone, so he stored it in there.

"If I don't see you at school on Friday, I'll give you a call Saturday to confirm," he said.

"All right."

He gave me a hug, and I went to practice. Nationals was about six weeks away, so we had our routine together. We just had to make sure we were in sync.

By the time practice ended two hours later, I was tired and sweaty. I rushed to take a shower so that I could meet Allen, who had started taking me home after practice.

Allen was standing by his car talking to his teammates I'd seen earlier. He looked mad about something, but I ignored it.

"Hey, baby," I said, kissing him on the lips.

He nodded to his boys. "I'll get up with y'all later. Thanks for the info," he said before climbing into the driver's seat.

I smiled at his friends, then quickly looked at the ground. Allen hated when I talked to them, but I didn't want to be rude, so I compromised by at least acknowledging them.

"You hungry?" I asked as we were pulling out of the parking lot.

He didn't bother to respond, but I knew he heard me because a few minutes later he drove to Milo's, a local hamburger place that has these really good hamburgers and seasoned fries. Come to think of it, they have good ice, too. It's kind of a mix between crushed and shaved. I can just eat a cup of it by itself.

Allen parked and we walked in to place our orders. Once we had our food and were seated, I dug in, but Allen was just sitting staring into space, clenching his jaw.

"What's wrong with you?" I asked, adding ketchup and mustard to my burger.

He finally looked at me, and he was so angry that I stopped what I was doing to focus on him. I touched his hand. "Baby, what's wrong?" I asked.

He snatched his hand away from me, and I frowned.

"You want to tell me what's going on?" I asked.

Allen flexed his jaw, took a deep breath like he was trying to calm down, then said, "Why am I hearing from my boys that my girl was outside the locker room half-naked and all hugged up with some dude?"

I looked at Allen and laughed. "Boy, what are you talking about?" I said.

"Did I say something funny?" he asked.

I picked up my burger and took a bite. "You're serious?" I said. "Why would I be hugged up with some dude in a place where I know your friends can see me?"

Allen got even madder. "So does that mean you're with someone in places where you can't be seen?"

I put down my burger, trying not to get mad. "What are you saying, Allen?"

"Don't try and flip this, Courtland. Were you or were you not hugged up with some dude outside the locker room?"

It really did take me a second to figure out what he was talking about. "Do you mean Nathaniel?" I asked, chewing thoughtfully on a fry.

"Don't play dumb with me, Courtland. Have you been with so many men that you can't remember them all?"

I snorted under my breath. "Allen," I said as quietly as I could, "you got one more time to come out your face accusing me of something. Nathaniel and I have known each other since kindergarten, and if your idiot friends had stuck around long enough, they would have realized that there was nothing going on between us."

"So why did you give him your number?" Allen asked.

I really thought seriously about whether I was going to answer him. I couldn't believe he was tripping over something so innocent. "Because," I said slowly, like I was talking to a four-year-old, "he wants me to tutor him in math. We're going to get together on Sunday afternoons, not that it's any of your business."

"You are my business," he said. He picked up a fry then threw it back down. "You know what? You've messed up my appetite. I need to get up out of here."

I couldn't agree with him more. I placed my half-eaten food back on the tray and threw it all in the trash, but I kept my cup of ice. I hoped that by the time he dropped me off, it wouldn't have melted all the way so I could at least enjoy that.

We rode home in silence. Although part of me was confused about why Allen was so upset, another part of me thought it was cute that he was jealous. When we made it to my house, I was actually kind of relieved to see my parents weren't home. Allen just sat there looking out the front window while I gathered all my stuff. Somehow my gym bag got caught on the emergency brake, and as I yanked it free, half of my stuff fell on the floor of Allen's car. I bent down to pick it up, but my hands were full between my cup of ice, my backpack, my purse and my gym bag.

"Aren't you going to help me?" I finally asked in annoyance.

Allen took off his seat belt and looked at me like I had asked him to donate his last kidney, then he bent over and started grabbing my stuff and putting it back in the bag. We both reached for the final piece, which happened to be my sports bra, which I had practiced in that day.

"Is this what you had on?" Allen asked, holding it around one finger.

"Yeah," I said, reaching for it.

He drew back so I couldn't touch it while he examined it, then he started pulling stuff out of my bag, throwing it back on the floor of the car.

"What are you doing?" I yelled, picking the stuff back up.

He pulled out my biking shorts and looked at them like they were covered in mold.

"You had these on today, too?" he asked.

I nodded, wondering why he was suddenly fascinated with my practice clothes.

Finally he said, "Don't wear it again."

I looked at him like he had lost his mind. "What?" I said, sure I had heard him wrong.

"I said don't wear it again. No wonder that guy was hitting on you. You were running around half-naked."

I started laughing. "Why are you tripping? You've seen me in outfits like this plenty of times."

He stared back at me, and I couldn't read his expression. "You're right, I've seen you in it. That doesn't mean I want all my boys staring at you, and I definitely don't want some 'friend' checking you out." He spit out the word *friend* like it was a glob of spit.

I just shook my head. "Whatever, Allen." I snatched my clothes from him and stuffed them back into my bag, then managed to grab everything and get to the front door. I had to set a lot of stuff down to get my key, and by the time I was opening the door, Allen was on the porch.

I didn't even say anything as I walked in. When I turned around, Allen was standing in the doorway, looking like he had something to say.

"I'm sorry," he finally said. He walked over to me and planted a kiss on my lips. "When my boys came over and told me you were talking to some other dude, I couldn't take the thought of you leaving me."

"I'm not going to leave you," I said quietly. "I love you."

"I love you, too, baby," he said, holding me close. "I didn't mean to sound so jealous. I just don't want any other man looking at you. Promise me you won't wear an outfit like that again."

I thought of all the bike shorts and sports bras I had upstairs in my room to work out in and started to shake my head.

Allen noticed and quickly said, "It's cool to wear it if I'm with you—that way I can protect you—but if not, I would prefer you wear something else." He looked at me with pleading eyes.

I thought about what he was saying. If it made my man feel more comfortable for me not to show my body when he wasn't around, what was the big deal? I finally nodded.

"Thank you," he said, giving me a kiss. "You know I love you, right?"

"I know," I said. I looked at the clock and realized my

mother was supposed to be home any minute. "You'd better go," I said.

"Can't I stay for a few more minutes?" he asked.

I sighed. I was still a little mad at him, but I didn't want him to go. "Okay," I gave in.

He followed me into the kitchen, and I began fixing us a snack. While the pizza bites were in the microwave, I sat crunching on my ice, glad that it hadn't all melted.

"What do you have planned for the weekend?" I asked after I had swallowed a mouthful. Now that basketball season was in full swing, Allen was practicing all the time. Sometimes Coach Patterson had the team at school as early as six in the morning, then at afternoon practice he'd keep them sometimes until ten or eleven o'clock at night. Recruiters were often in town trying to convince Allen to sign with their schools, even though he had already made it pretty clear he was going to go pro. I guess colleges were hoping he was going to change his mind.

He smiled. "That's what I wanted to talk to you about. I actually have Sunday afternoon free. Maybe we can go to a movie or something."

I was just about to say yes when I remembered my promise to Nathaniel. "Can we get together later that day?"

"I guess," he said. "What's so important that you can't spend time with your man?"

"I told Nathaniel I would tutor him in math, and we're getting together on Sunday," I reminded him.

"Nathaniel? Is that that clown my boys saw you with?" he asked, like we hadn't had the conversation earlier.

I nodded before I got up to pour Allen something to drink. "Yeah."

"So you want to see him more than you do me?"

I started laughing. "Boy, you are so silly. Of course I want to see you more, but I promised Nathaniel I would help him. He wanted to get together during study hall, but I can't do that because I'm helping you, and since he works most evenings, Sunday is the only time he has free."

"Where are you meeting?"

I shrugged as I walked over to take the pizza bites out of the microwave. "I guess here."

"Your parents are going to let you have another dude over here?"

"Yeah," I said. "Nathaniel's been over here plenty of times. I told you we've known each other since kinder-garten. We've had to work on class projects, and I've tutored him before."

Allen sat watching me get some napkins. "I don't want him in your house," he finally said.

I looked at him and sighed. "Baby, why are you tripping? He's coming over to study—the same way you came over to study."

"That's exactly why I don't want him over here. Studying was the only thing I could think of to get to know you better."

I blushed, pleased that he liked me enough to make up excuses to spend time with me. "Nathaniel's not like that," I said. "Trust me. We've been friends for too long for anything to jump off between us."

"They say friends make the best of lovers." Allen looked at me suspiciously. "What's really going on with you and this guy? You keep defending him like you like him or something."

I shook my head. "It's not like that at all," I said, then hesitated. "I mean, I had a little crush on him in elementary school, but that was years ago."

"So you do like him," Allen accused.

"Not anymore. I was a kid then. You know I love you," I insisted.

"Courtland, I don't want that dude in your house, and that's final," Allen said.

I looked at him and rolled my eyes. "The last time I checked, Donna and Corwin Murphy paid the bills here, and if they don't have a problem with Nathaniel coming over, then neither should you. You act like you don't trust me or something."

I had barely completed my sentence before Allen flew out of his chair and grabbed me around my upper arms. "Don't be disrespecting me," he yelled, shaking me. "Don't you ever roll your eyes at me again."

He was squeezing my arms so hard that tears came to my eyes. "Allen, you're hurting me," I said.

It was like he didn't hear me. "I don't want another dude around my woman—period. Do you understand me?"

I nodded, figuring that would make him let go of me, but he squeezed tighter. "Courtland, I'm not playing with you. Let me come over here Sunday and find that dude at your house. I don't want to have to hurt him."

He looked like he was about to say something else, but just then we heard the front door open, and Cory walked in talking about something she had seen on TV. Allen let me go, and I fell against the refrigerator. He calmly sat down in his chair and began eating his pizza bites.

"Courtland," Momma called out.

"In the kitchen," I managed to say. I smoothed my hair and tried as calmly as I could to sit at the table and pretend nothing had just happened.

"Hey, you two," Momma said when she walked in. She looked back and forth between us and smiled. "Isn't that cute? It looks like you two were having an argument."

I gave her a tight smile and picked up my cup of ice, wishing I could dump it on Allen's head. I couldn't believe he had put his hands on me again.

"How are you doing, Mrs. M.?" Allen asked, getting up to kiss Momma on the cheek.

"I'm fine," she said. She looked at us again before she focused on me. "Is everything okay?"

I tugged at my shirt, wondering if my upper arms were bruised. Thank goodness they were covered by my shirt. Before I could speak, Allen jumped in.

"We're fine. Like you said, we just had a little argument, but we're cool now, right, Courtland?" Allen didn't give me a chance to respond before he turned to Cory. "What's up?"

"Hey," Cory said. She had pulled out her PSP and was concentrating on the screen.

"Can I play with you?" Allen asked.

Cory looked at him for a second before looking back

down at the screen. "Nah, that's okay." She turned and walked out of the room. I wanted to laugh because Allen had really gotten his face cracked. It was good for him to see that everyone didn't worship the ground he walked on.

Allen got up and put his plate in the sink. "Thanks for the food, Courtland," he said.

I just nodded.

"Well, I guess I'd better go," he said.

I didn't bother to say anything as I stared at my plate.

"Before you do, Allen," Momma said, "I need to talk to you and Courtland."

He looked surprised, but he sat down.

"I don't know if Courtland told you, but she is not to have company when her father and I aren't home."

Allen nodded. "Yes, ma'am. I owe you an apology. Courtland told me that she's not supposed to have company, but I really had to use the bathroom, so I talked her into letting me in. When I saw her making herself a snack, I convinced her to make me some, as well. I apologize. It won't happen again."

Momma smiled at him. "Well, I guess it's okay just this once. You're lucky it was me who came in and not Courtland's father."

Saturday night I was hanging out on bebo.com, a social networking Web site similar to myspace.com, when Nathaniel called. I had pretty much kept to myself all day other than going to the game so I could cheer. Allen had wanted to go out that evening, but I told him no. There was no way I was ever going out with him again after his little stunt the night before.

"I just wanted to make sure we were still on for tomorrow," Nathaniel said.

I thought about what Allen had said about Nathaniel coming over, and I hesitated, trying to decide if it was worth taking the risk. Finally, I said, "Can we reschedule, or better yet, can you call Bree and ask her to help you? I realized I have a lot going on right now, and I don't think I'll be able to help you."

"That's cool," Nathaniel said, but I could tell he was a little hurt.

"I'm sorry," I said. "I really want to help you...but like I said, I have a lot going on right now." We sat holding the phone for a few seconds.

"Allen doesn't want you to see me, huh?" he finally said.

"It's nothing like that at all," I said, talking a little too loud.

"Yeah, whatever," Nathaniel said. "The Courtland I know wouldn't allow some dude to come between her and her friends. I'll see you around."

Nathaniel hung up before I could respond. I sat there for a while thinking about what he had said about Allen coming between me and my friends. Bree and I weren't really hanging anymore because I had been so busy, and after the games, I had started going out with Allen instead of hanging with the cheerleaders. Was I really allowing him to come between me and my friends? I shook my head, refusing to believe that was true.

I called Nathaniel back. "You know what?" I said as

soon as he said hello. "I'm tripping. You can still come over tomorrow."

"Nah, don't worry about it," he said. "I don't want to get you in trouble with your man. I'll just ask Bree to help me."

"Nathaniel, it's no big deal," I said.

"Courtland, I told you not to worry about it. Thanks anyway," he said and hung up.

I dialed Bree's number.

"What's up, stranger?" she yelled when she answered the phone. There was music blasting in the background.

I knew my number had come up on her caller ID, and I smiled. "Hey, girl," I said, using my cheerleader voice so I sounded chipper. "Where are you?"

"Getting ready for Jonathan's party," she said.

I frowned. "Who's Jonathan?" I asked, realizing it really had been awhile since I talked to my friend.

"You didn't get my message or e-mails?" she said. "I've sent you dozens of e-mails about Jonathan. I met him at the mall a few weeks ago. He's having a party tonight, and I called to see if you wanted to go with me. That's why I thought you were calling me back."

Hanging out with my best friend sounded like a good idea.

"I'll ask my momma and call you back," I said.

Momma asked me a million questions about the party, but since I didn't know Jonathan, I had to make up a few answers. She wanted me to get his phone number from Bree so she could call his parents, but I managed to talk her out of it. Instead, she made me get his address and told me she or Daddy would be there at ten sharp to pick me up.

I started to say something—most parties don't really get started until ten—but I didn't want her to change her mind. Instead, I asked if I could spend the night at Bree's. At least that way I would be able to stay out until midnight, which was Bree's curfew. Of course Momma said no.

I picked out some loose-fitting gray pants, a pink blouse and some heels, then took a shower and got dressed. While I waited for Bree, I checked my e-mails, which I realized I hadn't done in a while, and part of me wondered if it was so I could avoid hearing from Allen. He didn't know about my bebo.com account, so I had been going directly to it and messaging people from there. Sure enough, there were a few e-mails in my AOL account from Bree, as well as a few other people I hadn't heard from in a while. I started at the bottom so I could read the oldest e-mails first. It was so weird finding out about my best friend dating a guy through e-mail, especially when we went to school and had a couple of classes together. I had started eating lunch with Allen, and I realized that's normally when Bree and I caught up.

The more I thought about it, I did remember her mentioning the name Jonathan a few times while we were rehearsing her dance routines.

I couldn't believe I had been so caught up in Allen that I had neglected my best friend. I vowed that was all going to change. Before I could lose my nerve, I flipped open my phone and sent Allen a text telling him I never wanted to see him again.

Bree picked me up around seven-thirty. She was looking

cute in a short black skirt, a black and white top and some black high-heeled boots.

She told me all about Jonathan as we drove to his house in Ensley, and I told her about breaking up with Allen.

Bree got this strange expression.

"What?" I said, turning to face her as best I could with my seat belt on.

"Don't be surprised if Allen's here tonight," she said.

"What?" I yelled.

"He and Jonathan are friends," she said. "They've attended some of the same basketball camps."

"I'll just have to ignore him," I said, but I was suddenly nervous.

The party was dead when we walked in. There were only a few other people there—probably kids whose mothers had given them a curfew like me. The music was good. Bree and I sat dancing in our seats for about an hour before kids started pouring in. It was like one minute the dim basement was empty and the next it was packed with people backing that thang up, moving to the music and working up a sweat.

Jonathan came to get Bree, and they hit the dance floor. I took a quick peek around the room, looking for Allen, but I didn't see him. Before I could feel awkward about sitting alone, a guy asked me to dance. We ended up right next to Bree and Jonathan, and we danced through five songs before Bree called it quits. She knew she couldn't dance, so she just kind of moved from side to side, which would have been fine if Jonathan wasn't such an incredible dancer.

I was thinking about taking a break when a slow song came on. I tried to walk away, but my partner, whose name was either Luke or Duke—I couldn't tell 'cause he shouted it over the music as we danced—grabbed me and pulled me close. I caught Bree's eye, and she nodded her approval, so I decided to get through one more dance.

The song was almost over when I felt eyes on me. I searched the crowded room until my gaze found Allen's. He just stared at me as he sipped from a red plastic cup, and I looked at him for only a second before I turned my attention to my partner, who really did seem like a nice guy. I kept staring at Allen out of the corner of my eye, wondering if we'd get a chance to talk.

That was ruined when Bree came over and whispered. "Courtland, your daddy's outside, and he still has his police uniform on."

I groaned. The last thing I needed was for my father to come in the house, which wouldn't surprise me. Once, I had gone to a party, and instead of Momma and Daddy waiting in the car for me to come outside, Momma had come in with rollers in her hair and house slippers on her feet.

I said goodbye to my dance partner, pretending not to hear him when he asked for my phone number, then I grabbed my purse from Bree, who had gone to get it from a spare room, then I brushed past Allen without a word.

Daddy was outside writing a ticket for Jonathan's parents because they were serving alcohol to minors, then he got on his loudspeaker and announced the party was over. Kids were whispering and pointing at me as I got in

Daddy's car, and I slid down in the seat, trying to make myself as small as possible. I knew I would never live down the fact that my daddy had just ruined the best party of the year.

In less than twenty-four hours I had dumped my boyfriend and messed up any chances I had of getting invited to more parties. Could things get any worse?

eight

MONDAY morning I was getting into my momma's car so she could drop me off at school when Allen pulled up. I tried to pretend I didn't see him, but he honked his horn.

"I thought you said Allen couldn't take you to school today," Momma said.

I didn't know if I was madder at her for calling me on my lie or at Allen for making me out to be a liar.

As he got out of the car I rolled my eyes, and Momma saw me.

"Courtland, are you still mad at that boy?" Before I could respond, she continued. "Whatever he did, get over it. Obviously he's sorry." She nodded, and I looked out the window to see Allen going to the trunk of his car, where he removed a huge balloon bouquet. There must have been at least a dozen balloons with different messages like "I'm Sorry" and "I Love You" on them.

Although I wanted to be mad, I felt my heart melting a little.

"Good morning, Mrs. M.," he said before turning to me. "Hey."

"Hey," I said.

He held out the balloons, and I got out of the car so I could take them. "Thanks," I said. I headed toward the house so I could put the balloons in my room, and after asking Momma if it was all right, Allen followed me into the house.

"You deserve it. I'm sorry about the other day. It won't happen again."

"You said that the last time," I said, after making sure Momma wasn't nearby. She got out of her SUV and put my stuff in Allen's car, then she drove off, which she rarely did.

"Where's your father?"

I shrugged. "At work, I guess," I said. "I'll be right back." I headed upstairs to put the balloons in my room.

"What are you doing up here?" I asked. "I told you to wait downstairs."

"I just wanted to say I'm sorry," he whispered, walking over to me. "I never meant to hurt you."

I just gave him a short laugh. "That sounds real familiar," I said. "Didn't you say that before? Matter of fact, this whole little scenario feels like I'm experiencing déjà vu." I pointed to the teddy bear with the heart that read "I Love You" that was sitting on my bed. "Remember that?" I didn't wait for him to respond. "If I recall, you made the same promise about not hurting me after you gave me that bear. I can't believe I was so stupid." I went over and picked up the bear, then grabbed the balloons. "You know what? Take your stuff and go. I told you I never wanted to see you again. I know you got my text."

Allen looked stunned, like he didn't know what to say. Finally he just nodded. "I didn't think you were serious about breaking up. You can keep all that stuff," he said. "You're right. I shouldn't have put my hands on you." He walked over and placed a kiss on my cheek, not too far from my mouth.

"There's no excuse for what I did to you. I really am sorry, Courtland."

He turned and walked away without another word, and I felt my heart breaking. I kept telling myself that I was doing the right thing, but part of me wondered if I would ever love someone the way I did Allen.

The next few days were miserable. No matter what I did, I couldn't stop thinking about Allen, and I couldn't walk down the hall without seeing him. There always seemed to be some girl up under him, but the minute he would see me, he would push whoever it was away and try and talk to me. I really wanted to say something to him, but I didn't. I had to stay strong and not break down when I saw him.

I was combing my hair on Thursday morning, getting ready for school, and I decided I needed a change. I had been thinking about getting it cut for a while, and since my hair appointment was the next day, I decided to go through with it.

The next day at the salon, my stylist, Leticia, got real excited when I told her I was going to cut my hair. I hadn't bothered to ask Momma, even though I was spending her money. I figured what I did with my hair was my business. Leticia talked me into getting highlights, too.

When I got out of the chair a few hours later, I felt incredible. Leticia had cut about two inches, which was cool because I could still wear a ponytail if I needed to, and she had added these golden-brown highlights. She had flipped the ends up with a flat-iron, and my hair felt like silk.

I paid her, gave her a hug and promised her I'd be back in a couple of weeks. Momma had let me drive to the salon, and when I got home, she looked at me. I thought she was going to have something to say, but she surprised me when she smiled. "You look really good, Courtland. That style looks great on you."

"Thank you," I said. I looked around. "Where's Cory?"

"She's in her room," she said. She put down a cloth she was using to dust. "Allen called."

My heart sped up, but I tried to act unaffected. "What did he want?" I asked, hoping I sounded bored.

"He told me what happened." I looked at her and frowned, knowing that Allen hadn't told her what I thought he had. "Are you sure you don't want to get back together with him? He really cares for you."

I thought about telling Momma the real reasons about why Allen and I weren't together anymore, but based on her relationship with Daddy, she wouldn't understand. Instead of answering her question, I asked one of my own. "Why didn't you and Daddy ever get married?"

For a second I thought she wasn't going to answer. She

picked up the cloth and started dusting, then she said quietly, "He didn't want to. He said the fact that we were living together showed he was committed."

"What about you? What did you want?" I asked, sitting on the couch.

She looked at me and gave me a sad smile. "I wanted to get married," she admitted, rubbing the gold band she wore on her ring finger. I had overheard Aunt Dani telling someone once that Momma had bought it herself right before I was born. "As far as the law is concerned, now your daddy and I are married. When I was your age, I always dreamed about someone coming along and sweeping me off my feet." She gave a soft laugh. "I always called it the moment of impact."

"What's that?" I asked, wrinkling my nose.

"Just some silly term I made up. It always used to fascinate me how you can go along living your life and then one day you meet someone who in one moment just changes it forever."

"Moment of impact," I mused aloud. I really liked the term, but for me it had a different meaning. I didn't tell Momma because I didn't want to hurt her feelings, but it seemed to me her moment of impact with Daddy wasn't a good thing.

"Do you love Daddy?" I asked.

"Why would you ask me something so silly?" she said, suddenly taking an interest in dusting again.

"I just wanted to know."

She finally stopped dusting the chair legs and looked at me. "You wonder whether I do?"

I shook my head. "No, I think you love him, but I just don't know if he loves you."

"Your father loves me," she said so quickly that I wondered if she was really trying to convince herself.

"Then why does he treat you the way he does? You guys never spend any time together, and whenever he's around, the whole mood changes around here. If you ask me, he doesn't respect women. He doesn't even like me and Cory and we're his own kids. It's not our fault we're not boys."

Momma looked up at me in surprise. "Your daddy loves you girls," she said.

"No, he doesn't." I felt my eyes filling with tears, but I refused to let them fall.

"Baby, why would you think something like that?"

"He doesn't spend any time with us," I said, and before I could stop it, a tear fell. "He doesn't even know what's going on in our lives. Why does he hate me, Momma?"

I started crying, and Momma came and pulled me close. "Baby, your daddy doesn't hate you."

I didn't even bother to respond as Momma led me to the sofa.

"Your daddy's sick," she said softly.

I looked up in shock, mad at myself for caring so much. "What's wrong with him?" I asked, expecting her to say he had cancer.

"He's an alcoholic."

"What?" I whispered, shaking my head. "But I hardly ever see him drink—I mean, I smell it on his breath sometimes…" I shrugged, not knowing what else to say.

Momma gave a soft laugh. "He's normally out drinking when he's late coming home. There've been plenty of nights when I've had to go get him and drive him home."

I couldn't believe what I was hearing.

"Is that why he acts the way he does? If he knows it makes him act that way, why doesn't he just stop?"

Momma nodded. "He wasn't always that way," she said. "Your father was a good man. He was a good father when you girls were younger. I believe he still is a good man. I think the stress from his job just started getting to him. This disease has just taken its hold on him. I keep praying that one day he's going to want to stop."

"But—" I opened my mouth to speak, then changed my mind.

"Talk to me, baby."

"I just don't understand why he would even start drinking if he knew this could happen."

"That's the thing with alcohol. You don't know who it will affect. Do you think your father woke up one day and said he wanted to be an alcoholic?"

"No," I said.

"I think that's why I never started drinking. Growing up, a lot of people I knew tried to get me to drink, but something always stopped me. Part of me always knew that the road to being an alcoholic starts with one drink."

I nodded, never having thought of it that way.

"So why do you continue to stay with Daddy?"

"Because I remember how he was before he started drinking. Your father is a good man. The stress of the job just gets to him sometimes. Having that woman die during that robbery really affected him. He hasn't forgiven himself."

"So why does he take his anger out on us? It's not our fault. Besides, that was years ago. Why doesn't he just get over it?"

Momma gave this sad smile. "It's not always that easy, baby."

I sighed in frustration. "I still don't get why you put up with him."

She shrugged. "Love bears all things, believes all things, hopes all things," she said. "Isn't that what 1 Corinthians 13 tells us? I have to believe that. I continue to pray to God that your daddy will be delivered from his need to drink and bring me back the man I fell in love with."

"But why do you have to stick around and wait for that to happen?" I asked.

She grew quiet. "So are you going to make up with Allen?" she asked. I knew she was trying to change the subject, so I played along.

I shrugged. "I don't know," I said.

"What did he do that you won't even consider it? I know you care for him."

I was just about to tell her the truth when Daddy walked in.

He didn't even bother to say hello before he started in on me. "What did you do to your hair, and what's that mess in it?"

I tried to remember what Momma had said about him being sick, but he was already annoying me. I touched my hair. It took me a second to remember I had cut and high-lighted it. Before I could respond, Momma said, "Corwin, leave that girl alone. She looks cute. All the kids are doing it these days." I watched as she patted her head and realized she was starting to look older, like she had a lot on her mind. "Maybe I should go and get mine cut and colored."

"It'll take more than some scissors and some dye to help you," Daddy said, laughing. Momma looked like she wanted to cry. I felt so sorry for her.

"I think you should go for it, Momma," I said, trying to cheer her up. "Maybe you can go out and scoop you up a young man who will appreciate you." I couldn't resist adding that extra dig aimed toward Daddy.

She smiled her thanks and played along. "Girl, I don't need a young man. The next man I get, he's going to be able to pay my bills."

Daddy had been headed toward the kitchen, but he whirled around. "What are you trying to say, Donna?" he asked.

She waved her hand at him, but I could tell she was anxious. "Corwin, please. Courtland and I were just playing."

Daddy looked like he wanted to say something, but he continued to the kitchen instead.

Momma gave me a nervous smile, and I really wanted to ask her why she was with someone she was scared of, but I knew it wasn't a good time, and I didn't think she would tell me, anyway.

Instead I headed upstairs. My cell phone started

beeping just as I entered my room, and I saw it was a text from Allen.

I started to delete it like I had done with all the others he'd sent the past few days, but curiosity won out. It read: I LUV U AND I MISS U.

I thought about my conversation with Momma, about love bearing all things and believing all things, and I realized she was right. If she could believe that God would one day change Daddy, then I had to believe the same for Allen. I decided the reason that God had put me in Allen's life was to help change him into the man that God wanted him to be.

I picked up my phone and texted back. I LUV U AND I MISS U 2. CALL ME.

Allen came over that night, and he seemed a little surprised when he saw my new do. I don't think he really liked it, but since he was trying to get on my good side, he played it off.

We headed to Jim n' Nick's, a local barbecue place in Homewood, and Allen apologized the whole way, telling me how much he had missed me and that he was glad I was finally talking to him again. I was just starting to believe him when I spotted another hickey on his neck.

Allen saw me staring and tried to cover it up on the sly, but I busted him.

"What is that?" I asked, putting down a rib and pointing at his neck.

"What?" he asked, probably stalling for time.

"That," I said, putting my finger directly on the hickey.

He had this goofy expression on his face, then he finally looked at me. "Okay, I have a confession to make," he said.

I sat there waiting on him to finish. "I was missing you so much while we were apart that after you left Jonathan's party, I went to my boy's house and this girl was all over me. I was upset about what had happened with you, so she asked if I wanted to talk and I said yeah. The next thing I knew, we were kissing."

"That looks like it was more than kissing," I said with an attitude.

He took a deep breath. "You're right, baby. I slept with her."

My mouth fell open as he rushed to explain. "Really I didn't cheat on you. We were broken up," he said.

I was so hurt, I didn't have words, and although I told myself not to, I started to cry right there at the table. Allen looked like he didn't know what to do. "I'm sorry," he repeated.

"I was just missing you so much. I wasn't even planning on going to the party, but then Jonathan called. I'm sorry," he lamely finished.

"That was the night we broke up," I said. "You sure didn't waste any time."

"Baby, I promise you she didn't mean anything to me. You know how these groupies are always hanging around. Besides, it's not like you're giving it up." Allen kept on talking, but I drowned him out, ignoring my hurt as I thought about my promise to myself to love him the way it says in 1 Corinthians 13, just like Momma did with Daddy.

When he was finally done talking, I reached over and grabbed his hand and squeezed. "It's okay. I forgive you," I said.

He looked at me in surprise, and I laughed. "You do?" he said.

I nodded and picked up my rib. "You're right. We were broken up, even if it was only for a few hours." I looked him in the eye. "But we're back together now, and it better not happen again."

He came around to my side of our booth, slid in and kissed me. "Courtland Murphy, you are an amazing woman," he said. "I love you, and I can't wait to make you my wife."

"I love you, too," I said, and meant it with all my heart.

I had just changed into sweatpants and a baggy T-shirt for practice one day a few weeks before we got out for Christmas break when Allen texted me and told me to meet him in the gym.

I glanced at the clock and realized practice was about to begin, but I figured I would chance it.

"Hey, baby," I said when I spotted him sitting alone in the bleachers. I looked around, trying to figure out why the gym was so empty.

"Coach canceled practice today," he said as though he was reading my thoughts.

I sat down beside him, knowing it had to be something serious for Coach Patterson to do that.

"There's something I need to tell you," Allen said softly.

"Okay," I said, taking his hand. "Whatever it is, you know I've got your back."

He took a deep breath. "I didn't tell you the whole truth about that night at Jonathan's party."

"Okay," I said slowly.

"I told you there was one girl trying to get with me, but really there were two, and, well, the truth is, I slept with them both."

I sat there stunned.

"The one I didn't tell you about told me she was eighteen, but I just found out today she's fifteen."

"And how did you find this out?" I asked quietly.

He took a deep breath. "Her family is pressing charges. I'm being accused of assault and statutory rape."

If I hadn't been sitting down, I would have passed out. "What did you just say?" I asked, trying to take it all in.

He held my hand. "Baby, I promise you I thought that girl was eighteen."

I snatched my hand back and walked away. "Would you have told me if she wasn't filing a lawsuit?"

He shook his head. "Courtland, don't do this. We've been through it before. We were broken up. It's not like I cheated on you."

I didn't know what to say, so I just walked away. I thought about going to cheerleading practice, but I really didn't feel like it, so I packed up my stuff and caught the bus home. When I walked through the door, Momma was there watching the news and I saw Allen's face flash across the screen.

She just looked at me with tears streaming down her face. "Please tell me he didn't do it," she said.

I just sat down and joined her, and we watched the news story about Allen's accuser filing a lawsuit and watched footage of him being arrested at school. It must have happened right after I left. The girl and her family were holding a press conference. Allen sleeping with her was bad enough, but it hurt even worse when I saw she was white—or at least I thought she was white. Her face had been blurred out because she was underage, but they showed close-ups of the bruises on her arms.

After it was done, Momma just shook her head. "I don't believe a word of it. That girl knows Allen is about to be a star, and she's trying to get a piece of his money. Look at her. Why would he be with her when he's got you? There's no comparison."

"You're just saying that because you're my momma. You have to say that," I said. "My own daddy doesn't even want to hang around me."

"Oh, baby, it's okay," Momma said, hugging me. "Your daddy loves you. He just has a hard time showing it. Allen loves you, too. I know he didn't do this."

"Momma, he slept with her," I said. "He told me this afternoon."

Momma didn't know what to say, so she just held me while I cried. When I was finally done, she said, "We need to pray." She didn't wait for my response as she grabbed my hands and offered a heartfelt prayer. Once she was done, she squeezed my hands. "Everything's going to be just fine," she said.

I nodded, but I didn't really believe her.

Later that night, Aunt Dani came over. It felt like I hadn't seen her in months because she said she had been spending a lot of time with Miles, the basketball coach Allen had introduced her to, and she had gotten an apartment near Ross Bridge in Hoover. Whenever I talked to her, she sounded really happy, and she said things were getting really serious with them.

She looked different, too. She had on low-rider jeans and a simple top—as simple as a top could be for Aunt Dani—and some really nice boots. Her hair was done in a stylish bob. From what I could tell, there was no weave in it.

She walked over to me and gave me a hug. "How are you, Corky?" she asked.

Her words just made me cry, and when I pulled back, she looked angry. "I can't believe what this boy has done. Have you talked to him?"

I nodded.

"Well, what did he say?"

I told her about my conversation with Allen, and she just seemed to get madder. "I'll call him and talk to him. This is ridiculous," she said.

I shook my head. "Just leave it alone, Aunt Dani," I said.

"I won't leave it alone. He hurt you. He's not going to get away with it."

"I'm not going to give you his number," I said. I saw the old Loretta Danielle Dennis emerging, the one who could be extremely ghetto, and it wasn't going to be pretty.

"Girl, I still have his number from when he hooked me up with Miles." She must have seen the look of terror on my face. "If it makes you feel any better, I'll take Miles along with me. Allen needs to know he can't hurt you."

I thought about skipping school the next day, but Momma wouldn't let me. She told me I had done nothing wrong, and that I had nothing to be ashamed of.

After Momma dropped me off, I seriously thought about waiting until she drove off and ducking around the back of the school, but Bree spotted me.

Before I could say anything, she wrapped me in a tight hug. "Everything's going to be fine," she said. "I've got your back. I was at that party, and I'll testify for Allen. She didn't come until right before I left, but that girl was all over him and a few of the other basketball players."

I just nodded. When I looked up, Nathaniel was staring at me. He walked over and gave me a hug, too.

"How are you?" he asked.

I felt like I was about to cry again, so I just nodded.

"Good," he said. "You're going to be fine."

My friends surrounded me on either side, and we headed into the school. It was like all conversations stopped as I walked down the hall. I knew everybody was talking about me, but that didn't make me feel as bad as thinking that everyone was feeling sorry for me.

"You're here today," my teammate Rene White said the moment she spotted me.

I wasn't in the mood for her negativity, so I ignored her.

When Candy came up and asked me if I was okay, I started crying. Although part of me believed she was sincere, another part of me wanted to believe she was laughing at me in my face because she had warned me about Allen. When she tried to touch my hand, I moved back.

"Leave me alone," I said, glaring at her. "You're probably happy this happened."

She nodded slowly. "I understand if you don't want to talk to me," she said. "Believe me when I tell you that I wouldn't wish what you're going through on my worst enemy. I'll keep you and Allen in my prayers." Even though I didn't want her to, she reached over and hugged me.

The day didn't get much better. People just kept staring at me. It was all so weird. I was used to attention, but I hadn't experienced the negative kind since middle school. Finally I decided to skip cheerleading practice and went home and got in the bed.

A week later, not much had changed. I was thankful we were out for Christmas break so I didn't have to deal with all the kids at school.

I woke up on my birthday, which happened to also be Christmas Day, and tried to get excited. I was finally seventeen. I had been waiting for this day my whole life, yet I couldn't be with the one I wanted to share it with. I tried to pretend I didn't feel anything for Allen, but I couldn't just turn off my feelings like a faucet.

I went through the routine of opening my Christmas presents, and as my parents always did, they gave me my birthday present separately. A lot of people born on or near Christmas have to share their gifts, but my momma always made sure that I felt as though Christmas was my day.

I hadn't really asked for anything special for my birthday, since the only thing I really wanted to do was date, so I didn't know what to expect.

When I opened the small box, it took a second for it to register that I was staring at a car key. My momma smiled at me from behind the video camera she was holding, and I jumped up and screamed.

"Is this what I think it is?" I yelled.

"Why don't you go look in the driveway and find out?" Momma said.

I tore out of the house with Cory close behind me and stopped when I spotted the Toyota Tercel in the driveway. It looked like it was about ten years old, and it definitely wasn't what I pictured myself driving, but once I laid my eyes on it, I fell in love. I had my own car!

Momma, Cory and I climbed in. Daddy just stood there looking at his watch, so I decided to ignore him.

We drove around the block, and when we got back, Daddy's car was gone.

"Thank you, Momma," I said, throwing my arms around her.

She gave me a huge smile. I don't remember ever seeing her look that happy. "You're welcome, baby." She looked at me. "Do you really like it?"

"I love it," I said, really meaning it.

We spent the rest of the day just kind of chilling. Bree called and asked if I wanted to go to the movies later that afternoon. It was starting to get dark, and Momma wouldn't let me drive. Bree's mom came and picked me up, and we all stood around admiring my car so long that we were almost late to the movie.

Bree and I gorged ourselves on popcorn and other junk food, and as we sat watching the movie, I wondered why I had stopped hanging out with my best friend.

"That was fun," Bree said as we were leaving the theater.

"Yeah. We have to start hanging out again," I said.

She nodded.

"So tell me about this guy you've been seeing," I said as we stood waiting on my mother.

"I really like him," Bree said, getting this look in her eyes I had never seen before.

"Really? I couldn't tell," I said sarcastically.

We both started laughing.

"So have you heard from Allen?" she asked me.

"No," I said, kicking a rock on the ground. "He's out of jail, but I heard he's getting homeschooled for a while."

"Don't take this the wrong way, but do you think it's true what they're saying about him assaulting and raping that girl?"

I hesitated, and Bree quickly said, "I'm sorry I asked that. I know I told you I'd testify for him, but the more I've been thinking about it, maybe he did do it. I didn't want to upset you, but he was trying to hook up with that girl."

I shook my head. "No, it's okay. You're my girl, so you're probably the only one who could ask me that." I took a deep breath. "Do you promise you won't tell anyone what I'm about to say?"

Bree nodded. "You know I would never tell anyone what we talk about."

"He said they slept together, but he denied putting his hands on her." I hesitated. "I've been doing a lot of thinking, and I actually wouldn't be surprised if he did assault her. I'm not saying that he did," I rushed to say, "but a couple of times I've seen this side of him that I didn't like."

"What do you mean?" Bree asked.

I hesitated again, and Bree grabbed my hand and squeezed. "It's okay. You can tell me," she said.

I felt myself welling up. "He put his hands on me— twice," I said softly, and Bree tightened her grip.

"Why didn't you tell me?" she asked.

I couldn't even look at her I was so embarrassed. "Because I was afraid. I kept telling myself that he was sorry and didn't mean it, but…"

Bree reached over and gave me a hug. "So what are you going to do about it?"

"I don't know."

"Really?" Bree asked. Her question made me look at her. "Physical pains heal, Courtland, but what has this done to you emotionally? I didn't want to say anything, but since you've started dating Allen, you've changed. We don't hang out anymore, you dress differently… It's like he's got this hold over you. I think it might help if you talked to someone. Have you thought about saying something to your mom?"

I nodded. "I have," I said, "but..."

"But what?" Bree asked.

"She really likes Allen. I don't know if she'll believe me."

"Of course she'll believe you," she said.

"If you say so."

We sat there in silence for a few minutes. I guess we were both absorbing what I had said. I looked at my watch and realized my mom was about thirty minutes late, which wasn't like her at all, especially when she had to pick me up at night.

I pulled out my phone and called her on her cell, but it went straight to voice mail, which meant she didn't have it on. I called the house, but the phone just rang and rang until finally voice mail picked up.

We waited a little while longer, and when she still hadn't shown up, Bree called her mom, who came and got us. I was starting to get a little worried, but I tried not to let it show. When we got to our block, police cars and ambulances were everywhere, and we couldn't get through. That's when I really started to get scared.

Before Bree's mother could stop me, I jumped out of the car and ran down the street, praying that the flashing lights were at one of my neighbors' houses. I made it to my front yard just as EMT workers were rolling a stretcher with a body bag from the house. When I saw it, I lost it. I had seen enough movies and TV shows to know someone was dead, but I wasn't sure who.

I felt someone grab me, and I looked up to see my mother. She looked really scared, which scared me even more.

"Momma," I said, running into her arms.

She grabbed me and squeezed me so tight I thought she was going to crush my ribs. "I'm okay," she said, rubbing my hair.

I realized if she was standing there that only left two other possibilities. I searched her face. "Where's Cory?" I asked.

Her face crumbled, and I started crying even harder. "She's—"

I couldn't even make myself say the word.

She shook her head. "No, baby. She's okay." She pointed to a police car, and Cory was sitting in the back. I ran over to the car and threw open the door, then grabbed my little sister in a hug. When Cory saw me, she burst into tears.

"It was awful, Courtland," she said.

"What happened?" I asked, trying to make sense of all that was going on.

I held her to me, like I had done so many times before. "It's okay," I said softly, rubbing her hair.

I watched as the EMT workers rolled out a stretcher with my daddy on it. His shoulder was wrapped up, and there was blood on the sheets. I felt sorry for him, and I wondered if he was going to be okay.

"What happened?" I whispered to my sister.

She just shook her head and cried harder, then started talking so fast I could barely understand her. "It was horrible," she said. "I had just fallen asleep when I heard voices outside. I thought it was Momma and Daddy at first, but then there was this strange sound downstairs, so I went to see what it was and someone was walking out the back door. I started screaming, and Mommy and Daddy came running. The guy pulled a gun on Daddy, and Momma jumped in and tried to help. The guy shot at Daddy, but he missed. When he tried to shoot again, I knocked the gun out of his hand, then Daddy grabbed it and shot him." Cory broke down and started crying.

I stood there holding my sister, watching as Daddy sat up on the stretcher, refusing medical help. He walked over to a few of his friends who I recognized from the police force. He said something to them, then shook their hands. Most of them got in their patrol cars and left, but a few stayed around checking our house and looking around the neighborhood for evidence. Daddy came over to Momma, who had walked over to check on us. He hugged Momma, and for the first time in a while, I saw that he really cared about her.

He walked over to us. "You kids okay?"

I just nodded, then I turned to look at my sister, who was still upset.

"Am I going to jail?" she asked.

Daddy walked over to her and smoothed her hair. "No," he said. "We'll have to go down to the station and answer some questions, but me killing him was self-defense. You saved my life. You okay?"

There was something different about the way he was talking and looking at Cory. Normally he never really looked at either of us. I guess almost losing Momma and Cory was a wake-up call. I hoped it would last.

nine

The next couple of days were crazy as we tried to piece together all that had happened at our home. It turned out the guy who had broken in was someone Daddy had arrested a few years earlier, and the officers weren't sure if he was trying to get revenge or if it was a random break-in. He had brought someone else with him, but the other person had gotten away with some of our stuff, including some of our Christmas gifts, my purity necklace, which I'd forgotten to wear, some money Momma kept in the house for emergencies and Cory's beloved Sony PSP, although I didn't know why anyone besides us would want those things. I shuddered every time I thought about what would have happened if Cory hadn't woken up.

My little sister was still pretty traumatized by the whole thing. We were out of school for another week for Christmas break, and I was glad. Between what had happened at our house, which had made the news, and all that was going on with Allen, I didn't want to be bothered.

Cory and I spent most of our time playing video games. She had gotten a Nintendo Wii for Christmas, which hadn't been taken since it was in her room, and we would spend hours playing. I wanted to get more details of what had happened that night, but Momma told me not to force Cory to talk about it. She felt Cory would open up to the counselor Momma had gotten for her when she was ready.

The one good thing to come from the situation was that Daddy was home more, and he was actually interacting with us. The Sunday after the break-in he was dressed before we were and he went to church with us. Usually he was what Momma called a CME saint—the only time he went to church was Christmas, Mother's Day and Easter. I still didn't really trust him, but I admitted to myself it was nice having him around and taking an interest in us.

Aunt Dani talked Momma into a girls-only day with me and Cory, so the four of us went out to lunch at Johnny Rockets, a hamburger place near the Galleria. I was probably more excited than I should be. I figured the change of scenery would do us all good.

When Aunt Dani pulled up at our house, I didn't realize it was her at first. She was driving a Honda Accord, and although it was nice, it just didn't seem like something she would drive.

"Where's your car?" I asked the minute she walked over. Cory and I had been shooting hoops while we waited for her, despite the cold.

"It was stolen," she said. "Miles let me borrow his."

I looked up in surprise. "What is with our family? I can't believe you were robbed, too." I looked at the car again. "I thought you said you'd never be caught driving anything but a BMW or Mercedes."

She didn't respond.

"Dani, I didn't know you were here," Momma said.

"I was just spending some time with my nieces," she said.

"You guys ready?" Momma asked, walking outside.

"Yeah," I said.

Aunt Dani frowned. "Aren't you gonna shower or something? You've been playing ball, so I know you're funky."

"Dani, she's fine," Momma said.

I smiled my thanks. It wasn't not like Cory and I had been playing a serious game.

We all piled into Momma's car and headed to eat. Bree had been to Johnny Rockets a couple of times before, and she had told me the burgers were good, and she was right. After we finished eating, we decided to drive to the Galleria.

I was surprised when Aunt Dani didn't buy anything. Usually she had to leave every store with at least one purchase, but that day she just looked at stuff.

I stopped looking at jewelry and just watched her for a while as she checked out some gold hoop earrings. She really was pretty.

"Why are you staring at me?" she asked.

"My aunt Dani is growing up," I said, feeling like my momma.

She just laughed at me. "What?" she said, sounding slightly puzzled.

"Miles is good for you," I said. "You seem to be changing for the better."

She wore this stupid grin. "Yeah, I guess a good man will do that for you."

"We should all hang out together...." I caught myself. Allen had been released a few days earlier, but I hadn't spoken to him. I just assumed Allen and I were no longer together. I had thought about calling him a few times, but my daddy had told me not to. It's not that I really listened to him, but something in me just couldn't make that call to see if Allen was okay.

"You miss him, don't you?" Aunt Dani asked.

I just nodded. Suddenly I felt like crying. I had waited a long time to date and to find someone who loved me, and now that I had, it was all falling apart. I mean, Allen had done a lot of things I didn't really agree with, but I believed he was a good guy. Any time he put his hands on me, he always apologized. Maybe he just didn't know how to treat women. I mean, his mom wasn't really around, so he probably didn't know any better.

"Girl, don't let that man get you down." Aunt Dani leaned over and gave me a hug.

I nodded again, scared that if I spoke, I would really start crying.

She walked away from the earrings and glanced down at a watch in the display case.

"Now, that's nice," she said, admiring the diamonds

that decorated its face. She called the salesperson over, then after trying on the watch and debating for a few seconds, she pulled out her American Express card.

The salesperson came back a few minutes later empty-handed, and Aunt Dani looked around for her watch.

"Ma'am, do you have another card you'd like to use? The charge isn't going through."

Aunt Dani looked at her like she was crazy. "What are you talking about? It's an American Express. There's no limit on it. Try it again."

The woman started to say something, but turned toward the cash register. We watched as she keyed in some numbers, swiped the card, then tapped her foot while waiting for the transaction. A few minutes later she slid the card across the counter. "I'm sorry. It didn't go through. Perhaps you need to call the company."

"This is ridiculous," Aunt Dani said. I was embarrassed, so I tried not to look at her.

"Come on, let's go." We headed out the door toward the middle of the mall. As we walked out, the security alarm began blaring, like it was signaling what had just happened. Aunt Dani and I looked up in surprise, since we obviously hadn't bought anything.

"Come on," Aunt Dani said. "Those things get on my nerves."

She grabbed me, trying to pull me through the door, but I stopped. "Wait. We need to at least let them check us. I don't want them to think we're trying to steal anything," I said as a salesclerk walked over.

"I don't know why it went off," I said.

"It's been doing that all day," she said, sighing. "It must have some type of malfunction. You guys didn't buy anything, right?"

I shook my head.

"Go ahead," she said, waving us through.

"That was so embarrassing," I said as we headed toward the food court. I thought about my words as soon as I said them, and I hoped she didn't think I was talking about her card being declined.

"Wasn't it?" Aunt Dani said. "That's why I told you to come on. Did you see those people staring at us?"

"I tried not to look," I admitted.

I headed over to Chick-fil-A. "What are you going to get?" I asked.

"Didn't you eat right before we got here?" she said.

"Yeah, but I want a snack." Lately I found myself eating more and more, and I tried not to think about the fact that I had gained a few pounds. I figured I would work it off at practice at some point.

"What are you getting?" she asked, wrinkling her nose.

"Probably just a chicken sandwich and some lemonade," I said. "You don't like Chick-fil-A?"

"What is it?" she asked with her lip still turned up.

"Chicken—actually, it's the best chicken I've ever tasted. They do nuggets, strips and sandwiches, and I don't know how they do it, but all of them taste different. I can't believe you've never had it."

"Well, I guess I'll try it," she said, still not looking

convinced. She reached in her purse. "Oh, man, all I brought with me was my AmEx card. I've got to call them," she muttered.

"It's cool. I got you," I said. "Let me call Momma and Cory to see what they want. You know they are probably still in the video game store." I reached in my purse for my cell phone and as I pulled it out, a brand-new pair of earrings—the exact pair Aunt Dani had been looking at—dropped on the floor.

My mouth fell open in shock as she scooped them up off the floor.

"Corky, what are you doing with these?" she asked.

I didn't know what to say.

"Did you steal these?" she asked.

I could only shake my head. Finally I forced myself to speak. "I don't know where they came from," I said.

She laughed. "Girl, please. I was young once. You better be glad it was me who saw these and not your mother."

"Seriously, Aunt Dani, I don't know where they came from. I didn't take them."

"Then how did they get in your bag?" she asked, and I shrugged.

She sighed. "I guess we need to take them back."

My eyes got really big. I didn't even want to think about what the salesclerk would say when I took the earrings back to her.

Aunt Dani must have read my thoughts. "I tell you what—I'll take them back."

"Thank you," I said, relieved. I was still trying to figure

out how the earrings had gotten in my purse as Aunt Dani walked toward the store. I replayed the scene in my mind, trying to recall if I had accidentally brushed against the counter, causing the earrings to fall into my purse, but I didn't remember doing that.

The one thing that did come to mind was when Aunt Dani hugged me.

I really didn't have time to give it a whole lot of thought because I looked up to see Allen heading toward me.

I tried to ignore the way my heart sped up.

Aunt Dani spotted him the same time I did. I watched as she went over and wrapped herself around his arm, and they spent a few minutes laughing and talking before Allen looked up and found me staring at him. I tried to play it off, but when I looked at him again, he was grinning, and I couldn't help but grin, too.

By silent agreement, we started walking toward each other, and it was like everyone else in the mall disappeared.

"Hey," Allen said when he was standing directly in front of me.

"Hey," I said.

"It's good to see you."

I looked at the floor and smoothed my hair, trying to figure out how to respond.

"You don't have to say anything," he said. "I know you miss me, too." He lifted my chin with his finger. "You do miss me, don't you?"

"Yeah," I said.

"The charges were dropped against me," he said.

My mouth dropped open. "Really?" I said. Before I could stop myself, I ran into his arms, and he held me tight. It felt so good to be with him again. I gazed into his eyes, and I couldn't help but kiss him—or maybe he kissed me, I'm not sure. We just got caught up in the moment. It reminded me of the night of our first date when we had gone to the park.

Just like that night, we were rudely interrupted.

"Y'all need to get a room," Aunt Dani said, doing her version of a Southern accent.

I blushed. Aunt Dani was cool and all, but it still felt strange having her see me give my boyfriend a real kiss. I also remembered Momma and Cory were nearby

I smiled. Allen hadn't said anything, but I could feel he wanted to be with me just as much as I wanted to be with him.

"So, can I take you home?" he asked.

I looked at Aunt Dani to see if it was okay. "I am not getting involved in any mess," she said. "Corky, you know your parents don't want you seeing Allen. How are you going to explain him dropping you off?"

I hadn't really thought about that.

"I can talk to your parents. You know me and your mom are cool," he said.

"You forget you haven't been around for a while," Aunt Dani said. "Things have changed in the Murphy household. Courtland's parents are acting like they're in love now, and her father is trying to be involved in her life."

Allen looked at me for confirmation, and I nodded.

"I'll just call you later," he said.

* * *

I was worried Aunt Dani was going to tell Momma we had seen Allen at the mall, but she seemed to have other things on her mind. She didn't say much on the drive home, and I was glad. I was trying to think of how I could see Allen. I knew my parents wouldn't allow it, but that didn't stop me from wanting to spend time with him. I mean, I wouldn't be able to see him much during school, and Momma was back to picking me up after.

"Just sneak out," Aunt Dani said after Momma and Cory went inside the house.

"Huh?" I said.

"If you want to see Allen, just wait until your parents go to sleep and sneak out."

"But what if I get caught?" I said.

"Child, please. I've been sneaking out for years, and I've never gotten caught. Just make sure you're back before your momma gets up—you know she wakes up before the sun."

I thought about what she said, and I realized it made sense. My parents would only worry if they knew I was with Allen, but what they didn't know wouldn't hurt them.

Aunt Dani hung around until everybody went to bed, then the two of us spent some time casing the place. We walked into the bathroom that Cory and I shared, and she pointed to the window in there.

"That's big enough for you to use," she said.

I had never really paid the window any attention. "How do you know that?" I asked.

"Girl, I've learned to pay attention when I enter anywhere. You never know when you're going to have to make a fast exit."

"Do you guys think it's ever okay to sleep with a guy when you're not married?" I asked during the Worth the Wait meeting. The question had been running through my mind again the last few days, and I really needed someone else's opinion.

"Haven't we had this conversation before?" someone asked.

"So? I want to have it again," I said. "Do you think it's okay?"

"Why would you ask that?" someone said.

Bree looked at me, and I shrugged, trying not to glance directly at her, knowing she would know exactly what I was thinking. "I was just curious."

"If a guy really loves you, then he'll understand you wanting to wait until you're married," Jennifer said. "If he doesn't, then that's his problem, not yours."

"Are you kidding me?" Emily asked. "You sound like somebody's mother. Nobody thinks like that anymore." She turned to me. "If you guys really love each other, I don't see what the problem is. You're planning on getting married someday, so why wait?"

"She needs to wait because that's a promise she made to herself," Bree said, and I realized joining Worth the Wait had changed her way of thinking. Sophomore year she used to talk all the time about losing her virginity. "Who cares what some guy thinks?"

I held up my hands. "Hold up," I said. "I never said this was me. I was just asking a question."

"Come on, Courtland. We're not stupid. We know you're talking about you and that fine Allen Benson. If I had the chance, I'd take it. He plays ball, too, and you know he's going pro in a few months. He's about to get paid." Emily got this dreamy look on her face. "Think about it. If you had his baby, you'd be set for life with all that money he's about to make."

I had just taken a sip of Sprite, and I started to choke. Bree had to beat me on my back for a few minutes before I stopped. "Baby?" I finally managed to say.

Emily grinned and nodded like I had just told her she had won ten million dollars.

"Yes, a baby," Jennifer said. "That's one of the consequences that could happen if you sleep with a guy who's not your husband. Next thing you know, Allen will be running around calling you his baby momma." She looked at one of the girls in the group who had recently had a baby. "No offense."

The girl shrugged. "None taken."

"So are you thinking about it?" Bree asked.

"Maybe," I said.

"But why?"

"It's hard to explain," I said. "It's one thing for us to make all these vows when we don't have boyfriends, but when you get one and you're feeling all these things, it's hard. I mean, I really like—I mean love—Allen. It's not like he asks me for a lot. If all he wants is to have sex with me, what's the big deal?" I reached for my purity necklace, remembering a second too late that I didn't have it anymore.

"What do you want?" Andrea asked from the doorway.

"I don't know anymore," I said honestly. "I thought I wanted to wait until I got married, but it's really hard."

"But it's not impossible," Bree said. "Don't let Allen talk you into doing something that you'll regret."

"But what if she doesn't regret it?" Emily said.

"What if she does? It's not like she can get her virginity back," Bree argued.

"We're all going to lose it someday, so what does it matter when it happens?" Emily asked.

"If you feel that way, why are you a member of this club?" Jennifer asked.

"Because I told you, virgins are sexy," she said.

The room grew kind of silent as we thought about what Emily said. I couldn't deny the fact that Allen had me feeling a lot of things I hadn't really expected to feel, despite all that had happened between us.

"So have you thought about what type of birth control you're going to use?" Jennifer asked.

"Huh?" I asked, looking at her like she was crazy.

"Birth control," she repeated.

"Why would I need to worry about that? If I decide to do this, I'll just let Allen pick something."

"Hello," Jennifer said, using her fist to knock upside my head. "Is anyone home? Is it just me or did Allen not get charged with rape? I've heard she might be pregnant.

That would mean he didn't use protection, which would mean if you sleep with him, you're exposing yourself to all kinds of diseases." She shivered and puckered her face up like she'd eaten a whole pack of sour candy.

I hadn't heard the girl who had accused Allen might be pregnant, and I told myself it was just a rumor. I had tried not to think about Allen being with other girls, but Jennifer was right. If I decided to sleep with him, I couldn't leave it up to chance that he would protect me. I was going to have to protect myself.

ten

momma wasn't feeling well the next day, so I drove myself to cheerleading practice. Even though I had gotten a car, she still was slow to let me drive places by myself, which didn't make any sense to me. What was the point in having my own car if I could never drive it? When she called and asked me to stop at Wal-Mart and pick up some Tylenol Cold for her, I found myself staring at the condoms, wondering if I should buy some just in case.

What am I doing? I thought. *Allen loves me, and he knows I want to wait until after I'm married to have sex.*

I shook my head, then laughed, not believing I was even entertaining the thought of giving up something I treasured. I grabbed Momma's cold medicine, then got in line.

When I was almost at the register, my cell phone rang, and Boyz II Men's "A Song for Mama" came blasting through. I grabbed the phone, embarrassed, and pushed the talk button.

"Hey, Momma."

"Hey, baby. Where are you?"

"I'm at Wal-Mart. I should be home in a few minutes."

"That's fine," she said. "Can you stop and pick us up something to eat? You still have money, don't you?"

She had given me some money that morning. "Yes, ma'am. Is pizza okay?" I asked, thinking I could pick up a five-dollar pepperoni pizza from Little Caesars.

"That's fine, baby," she said, sneezing.

"Why don't you get some rest? I'll be home soon," I said.

"Okay," she said after a violent cough.

"Get some rest, Momma," I said.

"Ma'am, can I help you?" a woman asked.

I threw the medicine on the counter, and just as I was about to give up looking for my money, which I thought was in my purse, I finally remembered I had put the money in my jeans pocket.

"Will that be all?" the woman asked.

"Yes," I said, looking at the woman for the first time. "Andrea? I didn't know you worked here," I said to my Worth the Wait adviser.

"Hey, Courtland. I just started a few weeks ago.

"Will that be all?" she asked, and I wondered if she'd seen me looking at the condoms earlier.

I nodded.

She gave me the price and I handed her the money, waiting on her to say something, but she didn't. Instead, she gave me my change and said, "Have a nice day."

"You, too," I said, praying she didn't tell my mother.

* * *

Two nights later Allen and I agreed he would meet me at the corner down the street from my house after my parents fell asleep. Momma still wasn't feeling well, and I knew her medicine would knock her out, since she had had to get a prescription from the doctor that morning for the flu. Daddy was at work and wasn't scheduled to get off until around eight the next morning, so I figured I was good.

I tried to be as casual as possible when I stuck my head in Momma's room to check on her. "You need anything?" I asked.

She could barely keep her eyes open. "No, baby. I'm fine. I'm just going to bed."

"Okay. I am, too," I said, pointing at my robe for emphasis. "I'll check on Cory, then I'm going to call it a night."

"I love you, Courtland. Thanks for all your help," she said, and she was asleep before I could respond.

Cory was playing her video game, but I made her go to bed, and when I was sure she was asleep, I slipped off my robe, smoothed my jeans and straightened my sweater, then I glanced at myself in the mirror, praying Allen would like my outfit. He had criticized the stuff I had worn a few times, and some stuff he had told me I could never wear in public again, like my favorite Apple Bottom jeans, which he said showed my butt too much.

I headed to the window and climbed through like Aunt Dani had shown me, wondering after I made it to the ground why I didn't just use the front door. I giggled at my silliness, then headed to the corner where I was supposed to meet Allen. It was only January, and the day had been pretty warm, so I didn't think I needed a jacket, but I was wrong. It had gotten colder and I stood there shivering for ten minutes before I finally texted Allen to see what was taking so long.

It took him five minutes to respond that he was about ten minutes away. I thought about telling him to forget about it, but part of me really wanted to see him.

I had been waiting thirty minutes when Allen finally showed up. He didn't even bother to get out of his truck to help me in. Instead he reached across the passenger seat and flung open the door.

"Hey," I said, trying to hide my annoyance at having to wait.

"Hey," he said, looking me up and down. "Where's your coat?"

"I didn't think it was this cold out, and I wasn't expecting to have to wait out here this long."

"Yeah, I had to meet with some people," he said, not bothering to apologize.

"Where are we going?"

"I figured we could just go chill for a while."

"Can't we go get something to eat?" I asked.

He sighed. "I guess." He put the car in Drive, then sat there for a minute before putting the car back in Park. "Look, I'm not going to spend any more money on you if you're not going to put out."

"What?" I asked weakly.

He kept going like I hadn't spoken. "Look, with everything I've been through lately, I don't have time to play games anymore. You're cool and all, but I didn't think it would take this long."

"You didn't think what would take this long?" I asked.

"Getting you. It's been almost six months now, and nothing's changed. I can't always be spending money on you when I'm not getting anything in return. I knew I shouldn't have bet Noah—"

"You made a bet about me?" I asked, not believing what I was hearing.

He laughed. "Yeah. I remember when you were a freshman, thinking you were better than folks. That night at the fountain, I told my boy Noah I'd be able to break you. We bet ten dollars that I could do it."

"Why are you telling me this now?" I asked, feeling sick to my stomach. Noah had tried to run game that night, then had turned around and made a bet on me.*f*

"Because I'm tired of playing games. I know you don't want to be a virgin anymore. It's all over you. I thought you wanted a gentleman, but since you still weren't giving it up, it occurred to me that maybe you're one of those chicks who's into guys dogging you. I grabbed you and you kept on coming back, like a dog to his bone."

I sat there with my mouth wide open, not knowing what to say or feel. I couldn't believe what I was hearing.

"Why are you doing this?" I asked.

"Courtland, you know you like it."

Tears filled my eyes. I couldn't believe I had been so stupid. Allen had never loved me. Our whole relationship had been a lie.

He put the car in Drive and hit the gas, throwing me off the seat, since I hadn't bothered to put on my seat belt.

"What are you doing?" I screamed, trying desperately to find something to hold on to.

"I'm sick of these games, Courtland." He grabbed my wrist and pinned me close to his side. "They're going to end tonight."

"Allen, you're hurting me. Let me go," I cried as he drove faster and faster, driving through yellow traffic lights and barely missing a car before he jumped on the highway. He was going so fast, I couldn't read the road signs to see where we were going. I had never been so terrified in my life.

I tried reaching for my purse so I could dial 911, but I only had one hand free, and I was using that to hold on to the dashboard.

"Please, just let me go," I pleaded. "I'll do whatever you want if you just let me go."

He slammed on the brakes, then turned and looked at me, and as well as I thought I had gotten to know him, I didn't recognize this guy sitting next to me. "Why didn't you just say that to begin with?" he said, placing his hand on my thigh. It made my flesh crawl in revulsion.

He drove to a nearby school, parked, then reached for his belt buckle, and I took a deep breath. I had dreamed about my first time almost as much as I had about dating, and I never thought it would be like this.

Allen reached for me and placed a sloppy kiss on my lips, then he leaned back and reached for the bottom of his shirt and looked up at me with a grin. I used that moment to fire every ounce of pepper spray in the canister on my key ring into his eyes.

As he screamed in agony, louder than any girl I had ever heard, I reached for the door handle, bolted out of the car, then ran with everything I had in me, looking behind me every few seconds to see if Allen was coming after me.

I ran for what felt like miles, ignoring the burning in my chest, determined to put as much distance as possible between Allen and me. When I finally came to a stop, I had no clue where I was. I reached in my purse for my cell phone, only to discover I didn't have it. I groaned, wondering if the night could get any worse.

I started walking, praying I would come across a pay phone, but after ten minutes I still didn't see one. Finally I sank to the ground and started crying. I couldn't believe how stupid I had been. I thought Allen loved me.

I glanced at my watch and realized it was almost four in the morning. I didn't know where I was, and I didn't have any way to get home. I didn't even have my emergency twenty dollars, since I had spent it a few weeks ago when Aunt Dani and I had gone to Chick-fil-A. I thought about going to someone's house to ask if I could use their phone, but what was I going to say to them and to my mother when I asked her to come get me?

Instead, I just got up and started walking again,

ignoring the cold air and my icy tears, praying God would get me out of this situation.

My prayers were answered when I saw a car headed toward me. Before I could flag it down, the driver spotted me and pulled over.

"What are you doing out here so late by yourself?" a man asked.

Part of me was scared to approach his car. All my life, Momma had drilled into my head to never talk to strangers, and I knew I definitely shouldn't get in the car with one, but what else was I supposed to do? I just started crying.

He stopped the car and walked over to me. "It's okay," he said, placing his warm jacket around me. "Are you hurt?"

I shook my head and he led me back to the car.

"Want to tell me what happened?"

"My boyfriend and I, we…" I swiped at the fresh tears and took a deep breath.

"Take your time," he said.

"He tried to rape…rape me," I said softly.

The man sighed. "Did he?"

I shook my head, staring at the floor.

"Let's get you home."

"No." I looked up, my eyes wide with fear. "I can't let you take me home. I wasn't supposed to be out tonight, and I can't tell my parents what happened."

"You can't or you won't?" he said. "What's your name?"

I opened my mouth to tell him, but realized he might know my parents. "Courtland Dennis," I said, using Aunt Dani's last name.

"Courtland, I'm sure your parents are worried sick. It's a little over four o'clock in the morning. We need to get you home. Where do you live?"

"West End," I said.

"What are you doing all the way in Hoover?" he asked.

I shook my head. I was at least twenty minutes from home if I was driving. What he said clicked. "We're in Hoover?"

"Yes."

"My aunt lives somewhere around here. Can you take me to her house?"

He took off his cap and rubbed his low-cut hair. "I really shouldn't," he said.

"Please."

He started up the car. "Where does she live?" he asked.

"Off Lakeshore Drive, near Ross Bridge."

We headed in that direction and I realized I had stopped about two blocks from the 1-65 entrance ramp. I gave him directions, and we headed to Aunt Dani's. I just hoped she was home.

I had been banging on Aunt Dani's door for ten minutes straight when the man who said his name was Mr. Matthews finally convinced me she wasn't home. I slunk back to his car, trying to figure out what to do. The sun would be up soon, and I knew my momma would be awake any minute. She always got up while it was still dark out. Even though she was sick, that didn't stop her from dragging herself out of bed at her usual time for her daily devotion and to make breakfast for Cory and me.

Thinking of breakfast reminded me it was the day before we left for the competition in Orlando, and we really were supposed to meet at school early to have a celebration breakfast, sort of our last chance to bond before we got on the road the next day. Later that afternoon we were having a pep rally, then one final practice before we headed home supposedly to get a good night's sleep, but I had a Worth the Wait meeting.

The competition was really the last thing on my mind, but I knew I couldn't let my squad down.

I asked for his cell phone, ignoring Mr. Matthews's curious look.

The phone rang a couple of times before my mother, still sounding half-asleep, answered.

"Hey, Momma," I said.

"Courtland?" I heard a rustling sound and figured she was sitting up. "Where are you?"

"At school," I said, fighting the urge to look at Mr. Matthews and be busted for my lie and praying his name didn't show up on the caller ID. "Remember we have the team breakfast this morning? I had to help decorate."

Momma sighed. "I guess I forgot," she said. "Why didn't you wake me?"

"I started to, but you looked so peaceful, I didn't want to disturb you. I called Candy and she picked me up, but I was in such a hurry that I left my uniform. I'm going to see if Bree can stop by and get it," I said. "I forgot to leave you a note to let you know I had already left, so I was going to leave it on the voice mail."

"Okay, baby," she said, fighting a yawn.

"Okay," I said and hung up before I had to tell any more lies. I dialed Bree.

"Hey," she said.

"Hey. Can you stop by my house and get my uniform and a change of clothes? I'll meet you at school and explain everything."

"Okay," she said before I had even finished asking.

"Cool. See you in a few."

I hung up the phone, slumped back in my seat and closed my eyes.

"I'm sure you're exhausted after all those lies," Mr. Matthews said.

I opened one eye and looked at him. "I am," I said. "Can you drop me off at school?" I sat up, suddenly realizing it wouldn't look good if I showed up in a strange man's car. "Wait. Just drop me off down the street. I don't want anyone to see me with you. The last thing I need is for folks to start talking."

eleven

It took a lot of begging on my part, but Mr. Matthews finally agreed to drop me off near the school. I called Bree back to let her know where to meet me, then we rode in silence until we made it to the McDonald's two blocks away from school. It wasn't until we were pulling up that I remembered that everyone hung out there, but since it was early in the morning, not too many people were around.

Mr. Matthews cruised to a stop, and I reached for the door handle, but his hand on my arm kept me from getting out.

"I don't know who did this to you, but you're not helping him any by not saying anything," he said.

I opened my mouth to speak, but he stopped me. "I've got a daughter about your age, and I would be sick if some creep put his hands on her, but I would be hurt if she didn't tell me. Don't you think your parents need to know?"

"I'll tell them," I said, not sure if I really would. The more I thought about it, maybe I had overreacted. In all the time I had known Allen, he had never really done anything as crazy as last night. The more I thought about it, the more I tried to tell myself he had been drinking, but that didn't change the fact that he had wanted to sleep with me to win a bet. Momma said Daddy acted differently when he had been drinking, so maybe that's why Allen had acted the way he did.

"I hope you will," he said quietly. "I don't want to have to go to your father."

My eyes got huge.

"There aren't too many kids named Courtland," he said. "Your father talks about you all the time during our AA meetings."

"He does?" I asked, genuinely surprised.

He chuckled. "You girls have him wrapped around your finger. He would do anything for you, including kill anyone who messed with you."

Before I could stop myself, I started laughing. "You must have me mixed up with someone else," I said. "My dad doesn't care about me and my sister. He barely talks to us."

"Maybe he doesn't know how," Mr. Matthews said.

I thought about that, and it made me kind of sad. "All he has to do is just talk," I said, wondering why that would be so hard.

"Maybe he doesn't know what to say."

I started to respond, but I saw Nathaniel's car pulling

up and Bree hopped out of the passenger side. She looked around and I stuck my hand out of the window to get her attention. She spotted me and grinned, then frowned when she realized I was in a strange car.

"You adults have too many issues for me. Why wouldn't he know what to say to his own daughter?"

I flung the door open and got out, then stuck my head back in. "Thanks for the ride, and I appreciate your not saying anything." I added the last part for good measure, hoping he would keep his mouth shut.

"Hey, girl," I said, running over to Bree. I grabbed her arm and led her toward Nathaniel's car.

"What's going on?" Bree asked in confusion, glancing back at Mr. Matthews, who was just pulling off. "Why were you in that man's car?"

She and Nathaniel looked at me, waiting for an answer, and I opened my mouth to respond, but the words wouldn't come. I replayed the night before in my mind, and I wondered if anyone would believe me. Allen Benson was my boyfriend. Why would he try and rape me? Everyone knew he could have any girl he wanted, including me.

"I don't want to talk about it," I said.

"Are you okay?" she asked.

I nodded and Bree looked like she was going to say something else, but she glanced at Nathaniel and he shook his head, telling her to chill.

I raised an eyebrow.

Bree sighed. "When you're ready to talk, let me know."

On the short drive to school, I watched as Bree and Nathaniel joked around—not that they usually didn't, but this time was different. A couple of times she leaned toward him as much as the seat belt would allow, and when we got to school, they kissed.

"Woah," I said, shaking my head in amazement. "When did this happen?"

Bree grinned. "Officially last night, but unofficially we've been studying together for a while now."

"And neither of you told me?" I asked, looking between the two of them.

"I told you I was going to ask her to help me," Nathaniel said.

"And I've tried to call you," Bree said, "but somebody can't return a phone call."

"You know I've had things on my mind," I said. We said goodbye to Nathaniel, then headed toward the locker room so I could shower and change clothes.

"Okay, what's up?" I said. "I thought you were dating that other guy. What's his name?"

"Jonathan. Girl, we broke up almost as soon as we got together."

I nodded. "You remembered to bring a change of clothes, right?" I asked, taking a Wal-Mart bag from her.

"Yeah," she said. "Your mother seemed kind of suspicious. I tried not to say much." She walked around the locker room, checking to see if anyone else was in it. When she was done, she turned to me. "Tell me what happened."

"Bree, I told you I don't want to talk—"

"I don't care what you want to do. You're going to tell me," she said, sounding like my mother. We looked at each other and burst out laughing. "Sorry, but seriously, girl, I'm worried about you. Why were you in that man's car?"

"You promise you won't tell anyone?" I asked.

She looked annoyed. "Since we've known each other, have I ever told anything?"

"No."

"Tell me," she said.

It wasn't until that moment that I realized I had been trying to block everything out of my mind. Telling Bree forced me to relive the night before. Before I realized it, I was crying so hard I couldn't breathe, and snot was dripping down my nose.

Bree walked over and hugged me. "Oh, my God, Courtland. Are you okay? Did he hurt you?"

I shook my head. "I got away before he could."

"You have to tell someone," she said.

I looked at her like she was crazy. "I just did," I said.

"No. I mean like an adult. Maybe you should tell your mom," she said.

"I can't do that." I walked over to the sink, grabbed a paper towel, wet it, then started washing my face. "I wasn't supposed to be out last night. I snuck out of the house, remember?"

"You have to tell someone." She hit the paper-towel dispenser and I jumped. "Sorry," she said, "but I can't believe this. Courtland, you can't let him get away with this. You know what this means, right?"

"No," I said. "What?"

"He probably did try to rape that girl who was pressing charges. I wouldn't be surprised if he paid her off to save his stupid basketball career."

I shook my head, then thought about it. Had Allen really tried to rape that girl? "You really think so?"

"You don't?" she said.

We stood there in silence for a second, then I started changing my clothes, trying to distract myself from my thoughts.

I had just slipped on my pants when Bree shouted, causing me to trip.

"I know," she said. "Talk to Andrea. She'll know what to do."

I shook my head. "I don't think that's a good idea," I said. "She probably won't believe me."

"Yes, she will," Bree said. "She's always listened to what we have to say."

I slipped on my shirt, realizing Bree was right. Andrea had always been open-minded, even when she didn't agree with our opinions.

"I'll think about it," I said, then got dressed.

"Bree," I said, grabbing her arm, "promise me you won't say anything to anyone, even Nathaniel."

"Girl, why are we having this conversation again? I told you I won't say anything, even though I think you should press charges."

"Just promise me."

"Okay, okay. I promise." She gave me a hug. "I'm glad you're okay."

"Me, too."

I was headed to the locker room after the pep rally when one of Allen's friends walked up to me.

"What's up, Little Miss Unpure?" he said, and walked off laughing.

I looked at him like he was crazy and didn't even respond.

Cheering had worn me out. I had been up all night and after exerting all that energy for our routine, all I wanted to do was crawl into a bed, but I still had the rest of my classes plus a Worth the Wait meeting. I wanted to keep things as normal as possible. I knew if I skipped the meeting Momma would ask questions.

"So how was it?" Rene White asked as I was drying off. I tried to keep as much of myself covered as possible, but it was hard with the little towels the school supplied.

"It was good," I said, going through the routine in my mind. We had executed all the jumps, and the crowd had been on their feet the entire time.

"I'll bet it was," she said, grinning at one of the other girls.

"What are you talking about?" I said. "You act like you weren't there."

Rene looked at her friend, and they both burst out laughing.

"Am I missing something?" I asked.

"Not anymore," she said.

"You know what?" I said, grabbing my lotion from my locker. "I don't have time for this. Either tell me what you're talking about or go sit down somewhere."

"It looks like Little Miss Worth the Wait decided not to wait after all," she said.

"Wait for what?" I said.

"To give it up."

"What?" I whispered, feeling the blood drain from my face. "Who told you that?"

"I guess it's true," Rene said. She looked around the room and stood on top of a bench. "Ladies, I have an announcement to make." The room quieted down and everyone focused on her. "It seems our team co-captain isn't so pure after all. She's just confirmed that she and Allen hooked up last night." She and a couple of the girls exchanged high fives while Candy looked at me, disappointment shining in her eyes.

"That's not true," I said.

"Girl, don't try and play all shy now. You just told me. I don't know how you held out this long with that fine Allen Benson," Rene said.

She and some of the other girls started clapping.

I couldn't believe what I was hearing. I rushed to put on my clothes, not caring if anyone saw my body, then ran out of the locker room, trying to hide my tears.

Bree was waiting outside the lunchroom for me, and I couldn't believe how innocent she looked.

"How could you?" I asked.

"How could I what?" she asked in confusion.

"I told you not to tell anyone. Now all the cheerleaders think I slept with Allen."

"I didn't say anything," she said.

"Bree, stop lying," I said. "How else would they know? You're the only one I told." I turned to walk away, not believing my best friend had betrayed me.

"I'm not lying," she said, grabbing my arm.

Before I could stop myself, I turned around and punched her, and the force of the blow caused her to stumble into the nearby trash can.

I headed toward her, but a hand on my arm stopped me.

"Courtland, what are you doing?" Nathaniel asked. He pushed me into someone else's arms, then went to get Bree, who was stuck in the trash can.

"She told my business to the entire school," I said, glaring at Bree.

"No, I didn't," she said. "I told you I wouldn't tell anyone."

"So how do people know?" I asked. "You're the only one who could have told them."

"It wasn't me," Bree said.

The person holding me tugged at my arm and I looked up to see Candy. "She's right, Courtland. It wasn't Bree. Allen told," she said. "I overheard him telling a couple of his teammates."

I looked around at the faces of the crowd who had started to gather, and when my gaze landed on Bree, I had to look at the ground. Her eye was starting to swell.

"Bree—" I said, not really knowing what to say.

Nathaniel put his arm around her and led her through the crowd, and I turned to follow them, but a booming voice stopped me.

"What's going on here?"

I looked up to see Principal Abernathy standing in front of me. He took in me holding my fist and Bree's eye as she walked past us.

"You two, in my office now."

I had been in Principal Abernathy's office before, but not because I was in trouble, and as far as I knew, neither had Bree. I sat staring at one of Principal Abernathy's diplomas while he talked on the phone. When I heard him say my mother's name, I looked up.

"Why'd you call my mother?" I asked as soon as he hung up.

I knew I was being disrespectful, but I didn't care. This had officially turned into the worst day of my life.

"Courtland didn't do anything wrong," Bree said, and my mouth hung open.

"Well, how do you explain your eye?" Principal Abernathy asked.

I was wondering the same thing.

"It's my fault," I said.

"No, Courtland, it's not. We were just playing around. It's no big deal." She shrugged and sat back in her chair.

I wanted to give Bree a hug. We had been best friends for two years, but at that moment there was no doubt in my mind we would be friends for life. I had taken my anger out on her, and she still had my back.

Principal Abernathy ran a hand over his semi-bald head. "Bree, are you sure that's what happened?"

She nodded and looked him dead in the eye.

He looked at me. "Is there anything you want to add to this story?"

I opened my mouth to say no, but the more I thought about it, the more I realized I had done enough lying in the past twenty-four hours to last me a lifetime. "I punched her," I said before I lost my nerve. "I thought she had spread a rumor about me, and I punched her."

"Courtland," Bree said, looking at me like I was crazy.

I turned to her. "Look, I appreciate your having my back, but I'm not going to let you cover for me. Whatever my punishment is, I'm just going to have to deal with it."

Bree and I locked eyes, and I guess my determination showed, because I saw admiration in hers.

"Very well, Miss Murphy. As you know, we have a zero tolerance policy for fighting. You are hereby suspended for three days, during which time you will not be able to participate in any school activities."

I nodded, thinking I had gotten off pretty easy, until he spoke again.

"I'm sure your squad is going to miss you in Orlando."

My mouth dropped open. I had forgotten all about our cheerleading competition. "I can't compete?" I squeaked.

He shook his head, and he actually seemed as though he felt sorry for me. "I'm afraid not," he said gently.

At that, I burst into tears, and I sat there crying until my daddy came to get me.

I don't think he had ever been up to my school before. When he saw me crying, he gathered me into his arms and gave me an awkward hug, trying to comfort me.

We were silent for most of the drive home. "Where's Momma?" I finally said.

"She's still not feeling well."

"What's my punishment?" I finally asked.

He gave a dry laugh. "I think you've been punished enough. I know how much that competition meant to you."

I looked up in surprise. "You do?"

He took his eyes off the road long enough to glance at me. "Yeah. I was going to surprise you and come see you cheer."

"You were?" My eyes grew wide with shock.

He laughed as he came to a stop at a traffic light. "I know it's hard to believe, but I wanted to see you out there."

I didn't know what to say, so I just looked out the window.

"You want to tell me what happened today? Something must have really set you off for you to punch your best friend."

Everything in me wanted to break down and tell my daddy what had happened. He hadn't shown an interest in anything I had done in a long time, and as much as I wanted to share everything that had happened, I knew he would get mad and go after Allen.

"You know, you really can talk to me," he said. "I know I haven't been the best father, and I'm sorry. When that guy broke in our house, it made me realize a few things." He took a deep breath, then looked me directly in the eyes. "Courtland, I'm an alcoholic."

My mouth hung open in shock. Momma had told me the same thing a while back, but hearing Daddy say it was different. "I've started attending AA meetings, and I've learned that this disease affects more than me. I'm sorry for the way I've been treating you. I want you guys to know how much you mean to me. That could have been me in that body bag." He looked at me with tears in his eyes. "It could have been you, your sister or your mother. I don't know what I would do without you guys."

He paused, trying to compose himself.

I touched his shoulder. "It's okay, Daddy. Nothing happened to us."

The light turned green, but since we were in the police car, people just sat behind us, patiently waiting for us to go.

"But something happened to me," he said. "I realized that I want to be a part of you girls' lives again. I've been hiding behind my work and alcohol, using that as an excuse not to get to know you, but I'm tired of making excuses. Please talk to me. What's going on with you? It's not like you to get into fights. Even though the charges against Allen were dropped, I know this stuff has to have affected you." He gave a dry laugh. "I know I haven't helped matters. I'm your father. I'm supposed to be the first example you see of how to be treated in a relationship, but I haven't done a good job the last few years. I can't change the past, but I can start doing things differently right now. I'm really trying to change, baby. I haven't had a drink since the break-in at the house, and you know I've been going to church."

Someone behind us finally honked, and Daddy looked up like he had just realized where we were. The light was turning yellow, and we eased on through it and Daddy pulled over the first chance he got.

"What's going on, Courtland? Please talk to me."

I shrugged. "Just teenage stuff—you know, female issues," I said, figuring that would turn him off. Most guys hated any kind of allusion to menstrual cycles.

"Do you need some medicine?" he asked.

"I really just want to lie down." I grabbed my stomach for emphasis, and he nodded and pulled off without another word.

When we finally made it home, Momma was lying on the sofa in the den, and Aunt Dani was sitting there with her watching *A Wedding Story* on The Learning Channel.

"So what'd they do to you?" Aunt Dani asked, grinning at me as she threw the remote on the table.

"Dani, please," Momma said, rubbing her head like she had a headache.

"Girl, you know I want the details. I thought I was the wild one in the family. Now it looks like Corky is following in my footsteps. I've been training her well." Her face lit up, like I had gotten all A's on my report card.

"Dani, this isn't cute," Momma said, letting out a violent cough. She turned to me. "Why were you fighting?"

Everyone looked at me expectantly, and I just stood there. How could I explain everything that had led up to me punching Bree?

"Will you guys just leave me alone?" I screamed. Momma looked like I had slapped her. I ran out of the room, ignoring Momma insisting that I get back there.

As I closed my door, I heard Daddy telling her to leave me alone, and I breathed a sigh of relief. For the first time in my life, he seemed to have my back.

Exhaustion slapped me in the face the moment I spotted my bed. I had been up all night, and suddenly I was tired enough to sleep for a month. I climbed into the bed, pulled the covers over my head and prayed that when I woke up this day would be only a bad dream.

twelve

I woke up to the smell of smoke along with the chirping of the smoke detector and someone screaming.

Still half-asleep, I jumped up and banged my toe on the edge of the bed as I made my way to the door.

"Step back," I heard Momma yell.

I fanned the smoke from in front of my face and headed toward the voices, trying to figure out what was going on.

"Donna, help me," Aunt Dani yelled.

Fully awake, I ignored the pain in my toe and sprinted to the kitchen, my mind racing as I tried to figure out a way out of the burning house.

"Momma," I yelled.

"Corky, stay back," Aunt Dani yelled.

I stopped at the entry to the kitchen and burst out laughing when I took in the scene. Momma was calmly sitting at the table peeling potatoes while Aunt Dani, covered in flour, was standing near the stove wearing a long apron and oven mitts, shaking a fork at a skillet on the stove. She looked like a baseball catcher trying to get a hit.

"What's going on?" I asked.

"Girl, this grease keeps popping me," Aunt Dani said, almost tripping in her high heels.

"That's what grease does, Dani," Momma said calmly.

"Is the chicken burning?" I asked. I walked over to the stove, elbowing Aunt Dani out of the way to look in the skillet. It looked like Aunt Dani had just put a drumstick in there because it was still covered with flour, but the bits of chicken crust at the bottom of the skillet were burning.

I shook my head and grabbed the fork from her. "I'll do it," I said.

She looked relieved as she tossed her hair out of the way and switched over to sit next to my mother at the table. She picked up a potato, looked at it for a second, then put it back down and sat back and watched us work.

"Well, I tried to be domesticated," she said, crossing her arms. "My man is just going to have to accept the fact that we'll be eating out after we get married."

"You're getting married?" I screamed, turning toward her. "Miles proposed?"

"No, but I'll get a proposal soon," she said confidently.

"Can I be one of your bridesmaids?" I asked.

She shrugged. "I guess."

"Gee, thanks," I said sarcastically, turning to put more chicken in the skillet. "How are you feeling, Momma?"

"I'll be fine. I'm more worried about you."

Suddenly I remembered the past twenty-four hours.

"Girl, I thought you were never going to wake up," Aunt Dani said. "I went up there to check on you, like, five times."

"Why were you so tired?" Momma asked.

I looked to see if she was trying to catch me in a lie, but she was focused on the potato she was cutting up. "I didn't sleep too well last night," I said.

"Nervous about the competition?" she asked, and looked at me.

"Well, she doesn't have to worry about that anymore," Aunt Dani said.

I wanted to roll my eyes at her. Even though she was only a few years older than me and often acted like she was younger, I tried to respect her, but there were times when it was hard.

Aunt Dani glanced at her watch and jumped up. "I've got to run," she said. "I've got to get ready for tonight."

"Where were you last night?" I asked and bit my lip the moment the words came out. "I tried calling you, but no one answered." I prayed they didn't notice how nervous I looked about my lie.

"Girl, I was out with my man. We're going out tonight, too."

"Well, have fun," I said.

"Always." She grabbed her purse and was just about to walk out the door when she spun around. "Oh, I forgot to show you guys my new modeling cards."

She pulled a card out of her purse, which featured her

in a bunch of different poses and had her phone number, e-mail address and a Web site on it. I wasn't an expert, but I didn't see anything that blew me away.

"I think I'm going to try and get some gigs in Atlanta. You know they say that's the black New York."

"Sounds good," Momma said, sounding about as interested as I felt.

"See you guys later," she said. She blew kisses at us, then she was gone.

"Where are Daddy and Cory?" I asked as I turned the chicken.

"Your daddy took her to her tae kwon do class," she said. "Don't you have a Worth the Wait meeting tonight?"

"Oh, man. I totally forgot," I said. I had never missed a meeting, but after all I had gone through, there was no way I was going. "I'll just have to catch the next meeting."

"No, you'll go to this one," Momma said sharply, slamming her knife on the table. "Apparently you need it."

I jumped at the sound and turned to look at her.

"Are you ready to tell me what's going on?"

I gulped. "What are you talking about?" I started rearranging the cooked chicken on a paper-towel-covered plate to give me something to do. "Are you going to make green beans?" I didn't wait for her to respond before I went to the cabinet, grabbed a can of beans, then went to the refrigerator and got some chicken broth and bacon, which I started frying in a pot.

"Courtland, look at me," she demanded.

I turned to face her, still not looking her in the eyes.

"What is going on? You call here early this morning with some crazy excuse about leaving early for a team breakfast and forgetting your cheerleading uniform, then you get suspended from school for punching your best friend. I go into your room and your bed doesn't look like it's been slept in, a strange number is on the caller ID and the bathroom window is partially opened. Something's not adding up here. Did you sneak out of this house last night to see Allen?"

I looked up at her and my eyes widened in shock. "You think I wasn't young once?" she said. "You think I don't know you've still been in touch with him? Baby, talk to me. There's something going on with you I don't know about. I can feel it in my spirit."

I looked down on the floor, trying to find the words to tell her all that had been going on. I took a deep breath, but before I could say anything, the phone rang.

I lunged for it, but my momma stopped me. "Let it go to voice mail," she said.

"But, Momma—"

"Courtland," she said in her warning tone, and I knew to let it go.

The phone rang and rang, and after it stopped, it started up again a few seconds later. Momma sighed and snatched it off the hook.

"Hello," she snapped. She listened for a few minutes, murmured a few uh-huhs and said a few things I couldn't make out, then she glanced at me before finally saying, "I'll make sure she's there."

When she hung up, I waited for her to say something, but she went back to making dinner. "Who was that?" I finally asked.

"Andrea. She wanted to know if you were going to be at tonight's meeting."

"I guess you said yes," I said, fighting the urge to roll my eyes and neck.

"Go get dressed," she said. "We're leaving in five minutes."

"I can drive myself," I said with an attitude.

"You think I really trust you to do what you say you're going to do?" she asked.

I didn't bother to argue. I went upstairs, ran a comb through my hair, which was all over my head, and stomped downstairs, not really caring how I looked.

Momma and I rode to the church in silence, and when we pulled up, Andrea was at the door greeting everyone who walked in with a hug.

"I'll be back to get you when the meeting is over." I nodded, watching Bree hug Andrea. "You need to apologize to her," Momma said softly.

"I will," I said.

Bree had already gone inside by the time I made it to the door. "Hey, Andrea," I said, giving our adviser a hug. She gave me a tight squeeze.

"Hey, Courtland. How are you?" She gazed into my eyes like she really wanted to know the answer.

"I'm not having a great day," I said honestly.

"Bree told me what happened at school, but I want to hear

your side. I don't know if I'll be able to talk after tonight's meeting, but I want us to get together soon," she said.

"Okay." I really liked the idea. Bree's suggestion that I talk to Andrea made sense. I needed to talk with someone, and Andrea had always been cool and honest. I had a feeling she wouldn't spread all my business, and obviously she knew how to keep a secret, since she hadn't mentioned anything about seeing me at Wal-Mart.

I headed in and looked around for Bree, who was sitting off from the other girls. I slid in next to her.

"Hey," I said shyly.

She looked up at me. "Hey," she said and went back to reading her book.

"What are you reading?" I asked.

She closed the book so I could see the cover but then opened it so fast I didn't have a chance to see the title.

"Looks good," I said, not really knowing what to say.

"Did you come over here for a reason?" she asked, staring at me. I guess she had time to think about what I'd done, and now she was angry. I really couldn't blame her. Her eye had turned black and it looked like it really hurt. I couldn't believe I had done that to my best friend.

"Bree, I am so sorry," I said. "I should have known you would never have told anyone about our conversation. I guess everything that's happened lately built up and I took it out on you. Please forgive me."

She shrugged and looked down at her book. "I'll consider it," she said, glancing at me out of the corner of her eye. When I saw her smile, I threw my arms around her.

"I should make you get down on your hands and knees and beg," she said. "I can't believe you punched me."

I got on my knees in front of her and clasped my hands. "Please, please, please forgive me," I said.

A couple of the girls started laughing at us, but I didn't care. I realized at that moment that Bree was a great friend. She always had my back, and even though I had done something horrible to her, she was willing to forgive me.

"What, y'all a couple now?" someone said, and we all burst out laughing.

"She's not my type," I joked. "I like them tall, dark and sexy."

"Me, too," Emily said, and I rolled my eyes, not believing she was admitting to liking black guys. I had always suspected, but her words confirmed it for me.

We quieted down when Andrea walked in.

She smiled. "I see you guys are in a good mood today," she said.

A few girls nodded.

She grew quiet and glanced around the room. "I see a few of you brought in articles to discuss."

I groaned to myself, realizing I had forgotten one.

"Today I want to do something a little different. Is that okay?"

I sat back, relieved. Although Andrea wasn't strict, she did like for us all to participate, and I didn't like letting her down.

"Why don't we get a little more comfortable? You guys form a circle with your chairs."

We got up and dragged our chairs so they were no longer in straight lines, and once we got settled, Andrea walked over to get a beautifully wrapped box along with a Victoria's Secret shopping bag.

"How many of you hugged me when you walked in?" she asked, and all of the girls in the room raised their hands except for one who had come in late.

Andrea smiled and pulled tiny gold boxes out of the bag and handed one to each of us. I shook mine, trying to figure out what could be inside. Andrea gave really good gifts. Once she had given us all white fitted T-shirts with Worth the Wait written in black letters and she had been hinting that she was going to give us purity rings during a purity ball we were planning.

"Don't shake them," she said. I placed mine on my lap, as did a few of the other girls, although a few still tried to sneak and shake them.

"Who was the first one to give me a hug today?" she asked.

Two girls raised their hands, then glared at each other.

"You know I spoke to you when you came in, Lindsey, so put your hand down," Maria said.

Lindsey eyed the present and raised her hand higher. "I hugged her first," she said. "When you came in, Andrea had run to her car, remember?"

Maria lowered her hand.

Andrea handed the present to Lindsey, who bounced in her seat. "Can I open it?" she said.

"Not yet. I want you girls to open the smaller packages first."

"I want one," Kaya said, flopping back in her seat. She was the one who had come in late, and her brown eyes glowed with jealousy.

"Are you sure?" Andrea said.

"Yeah," Kaya said. "Who wouldn't want a gift?"

Andrea shrugged and handed a package to her. "I hope you like it," she said. "You can all open them on the count of three."

She counted, and we all ripped the boxes apart. Kaya was the first one to get hers open and she pulled out the slip of paper that was inside, read it and frowned. "What is this?" she asked.

By then, most of the other girls were staring at their gifts, too.

I looked at my slip of paper, which read "You've been given the gift of HIV," and I'm sure I looked just as confused as most of the other girls.

"Is this some kind of joke?" Emily asked, tossing her long blond hair behind her back.

Kaya threw the paper toward Andrea. "I don't want this," she said.

"Sure you do," Andrea said. "Remember, you made a choice—you asked for it." She turned to Lindsey. "You can open your gift now."

Lindsey hesitated, but then curiosity got the best of her and she ripped the wrapping paper off her gift. Nestled inside the box was a card that read "You've been given the gift of AIDS."

Lindsey made a face and dropped the box, looking at Andrea like she was crazy.

The room grew quiet as we all sat staring at Andrea, waiting for an explanation.

She looked each of us in the eye, took a deep breath, then began.

"From the time I was old enough to know what sex was, my mother always drummed it into my head to never have sex before marriage. She had me when she was sixteen, and my father was never around, and she didn't want me to get myself in the same predicament. Saving myself for marriage wasn't a big deal—until I got a boyfriend."

A few of us girls looked at one another, knowing exactly what she meant. If someone had told me a year ago I would have been thinking about sleeping with Allen, I would have laughed at them. There was no doubt back then that I would still be a virgin on my wedding night, but meeting Allen had made me question that.

"Paul and I met when I was sixteen. He was a couple of years older, but when we were in high school together, he was the cutest guy at school—star quarterback. I was kind of quiet then, and I had secretly had a crush on him for years." Her gaze landed on me, and as much as I wanted to, I couldn't look away. It sounded like she was talking about me and Allen.

"We started dating, and I knew I had found the love of my life. It wasn't until I went off to college that I decided to sleep with him. He was at a different school, and after it happened, he just stopped calling. I couldn't figure out what I had done wrong. I called him, and when I didn't hear from him, I got someone to drive me to his school, which was about two hours away. It took me most of the day to track him down, and when I did, he pretended he didn't know me."

Tears filled my eyes, and my heart broke for Andrea.

"I went back to school, devastated, trying to understand what had changed. Paul told me he loved me, and I believed him, and I tried with everything in me to figure out how someone who said he loved me could just drop me like that. I became depressed, and I was barely able to drag myself to class each morning. I'd come home and just lie in bed."

She sighed. "To make a long story short, a couple of weeks later I thought I had the flu, so I went to the student health center. They ran some tests, and a few days later I learned I was HIV positive."

"What?" I whispered. "You're joking, right?"

"No, I'm not," she said. "I've been HIV positive for about ten years. Now I've passed that gift on to you."

The room grew silent as we took in what she had just said.

She smiled. "Luckily for you, it's not a real gift, but I hope I've made my point. I got HIV from one sexual encounter. If it can happen to me, it can happen to you. Did you realize girls your age, especially black girls, are contracting HIV at the highest rate?"

"Really?" someone said, and Andrea nodded.

"I know many of you are in this group because someone forced you to be here, but I hope I've made you realize how precious your virginity is. Even if you don't have it anymore, you can make a decision today not to sleep with anyone until you get married. Abstinence is the only way to make sure you don't get AIDS or any other sexually transmitted diseases."

"You're just trying to scare us," Emily said. She threw her box on the floor and stomped out and someone got up to go after her.

"No, let her go," Andrea said. "Sometimes the truth scares people. She'll be back."

We sat there taking in all we had learned.

"Are you going to die?" someone finally asked.

Andrea laughed. "I don't plan to anytime soon. Listen, I don't want you guys feeling sorry for me. I have a good life, and I've learned to live with my HIV status."

"You don't look like you have it," I said.

"How does someone with HIV look?" she asked curiously.

I shrugged. "Skinny and sick," I finally said, realizing how silly it sounded.

"There are more people walking around with this disease than you realize. You can't tell just from looking at someone, and before you ask, you can't get it from hugging me. I just did that to prove a point. This disease is moving quickly. Like I said, black girls are the fastest growing population."

"That's because there are a lot of gay girls now," someone said.

Andrea shook her head. "It's black heterosexual girls who are getting it."

"You mean guys are giving it to us?" Bree asked, her eyes huge.

Andrea nodded.

"How will I know if my boyfriend has it?" she asked, and I wondered if something was going on with her and Nathaniel.

"Ask him."

"You can't ask someone something like that," I said.

"But you can sleep with him?" Andrea asked, looking at me. "Many of you don't have any problems making a decision to have sex, even when you don't really know a guy, thinking all you need is a condom, but condoms aren't a hundred percent. My boyfriend and I used one."

A few of the girls and I looked at each other, not believing that could be true.

"Does anyone have any more questions?" she asked.

"What made you decide to tell us?" someone asked.

"I saw a friend about to make a mistake, and I knew I couldn't keep this to myself. That's one of the problems with the black community." She glanced around. "No offense to my girls of other races, but I have to talk about what I know. We want to keep stuff buried and not talk about it. You guys are living in a different time and experiencing things I never even imagined. It wouldn't be fair to you if I didn't tell you what was going on."

"Thank you," I said. I thought about the night before, and as crazy as it sounded, I was glad things had turned out the way they did. What if I had slept with Allen? I knew he had been with other girls, and obviously he hadn't used a condom because of the pregnancy rumors. It was also obvious he didn't love me, since he had made a bet to take my virginity and tried to rape me. I was more determined than ever to renew the pledge I had taken to save myself for marriage.

"Well, I guess we've had enough conversation for tonight. If any of you have questions, please call me," she said as we started gathering our things. "Otherwise, I'll see you in two weeks."

The first girl was just making her way out the door when Andrea dropped another bombshell. "Don't be surprised if your parents want to talk to you when you get home tonight. I called each of them and told them exactly what I just told you."

thirteen

"SO how was your meeting tonight?" Momma asked on the drive home.

"It was good," I said.

"Anything happen you want to talk to me about?"

I sat looking out the window.

"Well?" she asked when I didn't say anything after a few seconds.

"Andrea is HIV positive," I said softly.

"I know. I'm really sorry to hear it. When she told me earlier, I was so shocked I couldn't say anything. I thought about telling you, but I figured you should hear it from her."

I just kept staring out the window.

When Momma swung into the parking lot of Ben and Jerry's, I looked up in surprise. "We need some girl time," she said.

I got out of the car without a word and we went inside. After we had gotten our ice cream, we sat in the car, eating in silence.

"We should do this more often," Momma said when she was done.

"No, we shouldn't," I said. "There's no way I want to go back to the old Courtland." I got a mental picture of me being fat, and shuddered.

"What was so wrong with the old Courtland?"

"I was fat," I said. "No one liked me back then. Everybody thought I was stuck-up because I was too shy to say anything to anyone."

"No one like who? Allen?" she said.

I nodded. "It wasn't just him. There were a lot of kids who wouldn't think of talking to me back then. Now we're friends."

"Are you really?" Momma asked.

"Yeah," I said, but suddenly I wasn't so sure. A lot of the kids I thought I was cool with really hadn't had much to say to me, especially after they found out Allen and I had broken up.

"What about Bree?" she asked. She saw someone she knew going into Ben and Jerry's and smiled, then turned back to me.

"Bree's always been my friend. She'll always be my friend," I said.

"I think so, too, but what makes you say that?"

I shrugged. "She just has my back," I said. "I can talk to her about anything, and I don't have to worry she's going to run and tell someone."

"Do you think that's true of me?"

"Sometimes," I said, not really wanting to hurt her

feelings. "I talk to you about most things, but there are a few things I don't think you would understand."

"Like what?" she said.

"I did sneak out to see Allen last night," I said, not believing I had let the words come out.

I waited for Momma to start yelling and screaming, but she just calmly sat there. "Do you want to tell me what happened?"

I started replaying the night before in my mind, and it just became too much. The tears started gushing out.

"Oh, Courtland," Momma said, reaching out to hug me. "What did you do?"

"What makes you think I did something?" I asked, pulling back to look at her.

"Why else would you be acting this way if you hadn't slept with him?" she said.

I laughed under my breath as I dried my tears with the sleeve of my shirt. "I don't know, Momma," I said. I was suddenly glad she hadn't let me finish the story. Obviously she wasn't going to believe me anyway. She had already made up her mind that I had done something wrong.

She stared at me for a few seconds, but I refused to look at her. "Courtland, please talk to me," she said. "I'm sorry for making assumptions. Tell me what happened. I can't help you if you don't tell me."

"Nothing happened, Momma," I said dryly.

"Are you sure?" she said.

"Positive. Can we go?"

She sighed and started the car. When we pulled into the

driveway, I reached for the door handle, and she grabbed my arm. I jerked away from her, her touch reminding me of the time Allen had grabbed me.

"What's your problem?" she asked.

With everything in me I wanted to say "you," but I knew if I did there was no way I would make it out of the car alive. "I'm just tired," I said.

"Courtland, I know you might not think you can talk to me, but you can. If you won't open up to me, please talk to someone."

"Okay, I'll talk to Aunt Dani," I said, just to get her to stop talking.

I saw Momma shaking her head out of the corner of my eye. "I'd prefer you find someone else. How about Andrea?"

I looked at her. "Why can't I talk to Aunt Dani?"

"I just don't think she has the best judgment," she said. "She's pretty immature for her age, and she hangs around too many men—at least she used to. I don't want her influencing you."

"But she's your sister," I said.

"We're half sisters," she said. "Our mothers had totally different ways of parenting. You know your grandmother didn't play."

I nodded and laughed. "I remember all those stories she used to tell about you getting into trouble while you were growing up. You spent a lot of time on punishment."

Momma laughed and shook her head. "It wasn't punishment. I was getting my behind beat, and not just by my parents. Back then everybody could beat you—teachers, principals, neighbors, the drunk on the street. Then you'd get beat when you got home. I promised myself I would never do that to my own kids."

"But you whipped me when I was younger," I said.

"Yeah, that's true. You'll learn when you become a mother that you find yourself doing a lot of things you never thought you would do."

"Does that include getting married?" I asked.

"Yeah, including marriage," Momma said, sounding a little sad. "I always thought I would have this huge wedding. All my friends would be bridesmaids.... That wasn't meant to be."

"Why not?" I asked.

"To be honest with you, it's because I didn't love myself enough. I loved your father, but he didn't want to get married, and instead of just walking away or demanding that he do right by me, I decided to settle for what he was willing to give."

"Why don't you walk away now?" I asked, really wanting to know.

"You kids are a big part of it, but honestly, I love your father. For a while things were rough between us, but since the break-in, they've gotten much better. We have the relationship I've been praying for for years. He's going to church with us now, and he's even put in to have his shift changed so he can spend more time with us. He's attending AA, and I've been thinking maybe you, your sister and I should go to Al-Anon."

"What's that?"

"It's a support group for the families of alcoholics."

"You really think we should go?" I asked.

"I really do," she said. "He wants to be involved in our lives now. We just have to let him."

"I would like that," I said, realizing I meant it. Daddy and I didn't have the relationship we once had, but it was better than it used to be.

"I would, too," she said.

"So do you love yourself now?" I asked.

"I'm getting there," she said without hesitation.

"So why don't you demand he marry you?"

She looked surprised at my question. "I guess I really hadn't thought about it. I'm so used to how things are, but you're right—you have to teach people how to treat you."

"What does that mean?" I asked, wrinkling my nose.

"It means people will do to you what you allow. If someone curses at you and you don't say anything about it, they are going to curse at you again. If they hit you and you don't say anything, they'll hit you again. By not doing anything, you've taught them that what they're doing is acceptable."

I thought about what she said and realized she was right. Although I had said something to Allen the first time he put his hands on me, when I had taken him back, I had taught him that I was willing to accept that type of behavior, which was why he kept getting worse and worse. I made up my mind right then it would never happen again.

"Do you love yourself?" Momma asked, staring at me.

"I'm getting there, too," I said.

She looked like she wanted to say something, but she hesitated. "If there's anything I can do to help you get there, let me know."

I nodded. "I will."

"I love you, Courtland, and I'm really proud of you."

"What have I done for you to be proud of?" I asked.

"You've always been a good kid. Now look at you. This time next year you'll be getting ready to graduate from high school." Her eyes filled with tears. "It seems like just yesterday you were starting school."

"Momma," I whined. Every now and then she would get sentimental, and it normally didn't bother me, but with all that had happened over the last day, I couldn't deal with anything else so heavy.

I didn't even bother to change into my pajamas before I climbed into bed that night. When I woke up, the sun was shining bright, and I was shocked to see it was almost one o'clock in the afternoon.

I jumped up, thinking I was late for school, but then I remembered my suspension. I went to the bathroom and was headed downstairs to get something to eat when my cell phone beeped, indicating I had new messages.

Aunt Dani had surprised me with a new phone just like hers that allowed you to surf the Internet and do video e-mails because she said she couldn't have her niece walking around with a bootleg prepaid phone. It was nice, but I didn't think it was worth all the money she had paid. I mainly just used it for texting and checking my e-mail. She had paid the bill on the first couple of months, but then she told me I had to pay it. I was thinking about going back to my prepaid one because I couldn't afford the monthly bill.

I had ten voice messages when I checked.

"Courtland, we won," Candy yelled into my voice mail. I could barely hear her for all the noise in the background.

"For real?" I said before I realized she wasn't really on the phone. I started jumping around, excited for my team, even if I couldn't be there. They'd flown to Orlando early that morning, and it looked like they weren't playing about handling their business.

We would be recognized as state champions for the next year, and as cheerleading co-captain, I couldn't help but be proud. There was a good chance I would be voted captain next year, since Candy was graduating, and our team would have major bragging rights. But the more I thought about the cheerleading squad, the more I was starting to question the idea of being a member of the squad at all next year. I had come to enjoy it, but I thought about what Momma had said about learning to love yourself. I realized in order to do that, I had to be true to myself, and truthfully, I wanted to play basketball.

I was only half listening to the next message when it started to play, and after hearing it I frowned and replayed it.

"Hey, baby, I was just calling to check on you—make sure you were okay after our argument the other day. I was hoping we could get together tonight."

"I can't believe this boy had the nerve to call me," I

muttered, listening to Allen's message one more time. I tried to ignore the way his voice sent chills down my spine.

I listened to the other messages as I tried to figure out whether I should call him back. He had left three more messages, and in each one he sounded a little sadder.

He had also texted me a couple of times. I had just put down the phone when it rang. Before I could stop myself, I answered it, and I was relieved when I realized it wasn't Allen.

"Courtland," a male voice said.

"Yes?"

"This is Miles."

"Oh, hey," I said to Aunt Dani's boyfriend. "How'd you get my number?"

"I had to sneak and get it out of your aunt's phone," he said. "I hope you don't mind. I really need your help."

"Okay," I said. "What's up?"

"I want you to help me pick out an engagement ring for your aunt."

"For real?" I squealed.

"Yeah. My boss and I are in town today. Can you go with me?"

"Sure," I said, then I realized since I had been suspended from school, I probably wasn't supposed to leave the house. "Wait, I have to ask my momma. Can I call you back in a few minutes?"

"That's fine," he said. He gave me his number and I quickly called Momma at work.

"Hey, Momma," I said.

"Hey, baby. You sound like you're in a good mood."

"I am. Miles just called and asked me to go with him to help pick out an engagement ring for Aunt Dani."

"Why didn't he ask me?" she said, sounding hurt.

"Because you're old," I joked.

"Ha, ha."

"Can I go?" When she hesitated, I threw in, "Please, Momma. How often do people get engaged? This is the chance of a lifetime. I know I got suspended, and I promise when Miles and I get back, I'll stay in the house until you tell me I can come out." I knew I was pushing it, but I really wanted to go.

Momma laughed. "You sure are spreading it on thick. I guess it will be okay. What's Miles's number?"

"Momma," I said, "stop treating me like a baby."

"Courtland, we don't know this man all that well. We've only met him a couple of times. I want to be able to get in touch with him."

I gave her the number, then quickly called Miles back. He told me he would come get me in half an hour, so I rushed to shower and get dressed. I was just tying the laces on my Air Force Ones when he rang the doorbell.

"Hey, Miles," I said, letting him in. "Just let me grab my purse and I'll be ready."

"Wait," he said, grabbing my arm. "I want to get your opinion on this ring."

He reached into his pocket, and I frowned. "I thought we were going to pick one out," I said.

He laughed. "We are. I found a picture of one that I

really like, and I wanted to see what you thought. If you don't like it, you can go with me to the mall."

Miles pulled a folded page from a magazine out of his pocket and handed it to me.

The diamond was nice, and most women would have loved it, but Aunt Dani wasn't most women. Although the ring looked like it was about a carat, I knew Aunt Dani would want at least three times that size. "This is the one you're thinking about getting?" I asked, pointing to it to make sure.

"Yeah," he said defensively, "what's wrong with it?"

"Uh, Miles, I'm no expert, but it looks a little small."

"You don't think your aunt will like it?" he asked. "I picked it because it's what I can afford."

"That's all you can afford?" I asked, trying to hide my surprise. Aunt Dani had been doing all this talk about how he could afford to buy her just about anything, but he was cheap.

"Yeah," he said. "I don't make a lot of money as a coach."

"Are you sure Aunt Dani knows that?" I said.

"Of course I'm sure. We've had this conversation a lot. She says she loves me because of the way I make her feel, not because of my bank account."

"That's sweet," I said, wondering if we were talking about the same person.

"You really think she'd like something bigger?"

I nodded. "Well, why don't you show me some rings you think she'd like, and I'll see what I can do?"

"Okay. Let me grab my stuff."

I ran upstairs, and when I came back down, Miles was walking around the living room looking at our family pictures. "You and Loretta look so much alike," he said. "You could almost pass for twins."

It took me a minute to realize he meant Aunt Dani, since no one called her Loretta.

"A couple of other people have said that, too," I said. "I don't really see the resemblance."

"Really?" he said.

I shrugged. "You ready?"

He stared at the picture for a few more minutes. "You both even have the same necklace," he said, pointing to one of the pictures.

I tried to recall which necklace we had alike, but I couldn't, so I walked over to the picture. "Which necklace?" I said.

He tapped a photo of me taken last Easter Sunday where I was wearing a new dress and my Worth the Wait necklace.

"Aunt Dani doesn't have one of those," I said. "That's my purity necklace. Only the members of my virgin club have them."

"Yes, she does," he said. "I took a picture of her wearing it a couple of weeks ago." He pulled out his cell phone and the screensaver was a photo of Aunt Dani wearing a necklace that looked just like mine. I stared at the picture, trying to figure out where she could have gotten the necklace, since we had special ordered them and each one had been personalized with our initials and the date we had received it.

"Now that I think about it," Miles said like he was reading my thoughts, "the clasp must have been loose on it or something because it fell off one day when she was at my house. When I picked it up, I asked about the inscription on it, and she said she had borrowed it from you."

I frowned. "When was this?" I asked.

"In January," he said. "I remember because it was the day after my birthday."

I felt like I was going to pass out. "When is your birthday?" I asked.

"January sixth."

My heart sped up. The robbery had happened Christmas Day. I stood there in shock, trying to tell myself that my aunt had not broken in to my house and stolen my necklace along with a bunch of other stuff.

I shook my head, trying to make sense of everything. That's when I happened to glance at the picture of Aunt Dani on Miles's cell phone and noticed her earrings. They looked just like the ones she had accused me of stealing at the mall—the gold hoops she had promised me she was going to return.

"Miles, I'm not feeling too well," I said. I felt nauseated, and I struggled to make my way to the couch.

Miles grabbed my arm and helped me to sit down. I pointed him in the general direction of the kitchen and he rushed off to get me a glass of water.

"What's going on?" I muttered. I still had Miles's cell phone, and I just kept staring at the picture, hoping there was some mistake. I thought back to the night of the burglary. The guy who was killed was someone who knew Daddy. The police had suspected there were two people in the house. Could it have been Aunt Dani?

Miles handed me the glass of water, and I took a sip, but it hurt to swallow. "Miles," I said, "what did the inscription on the necklace say?"

"It was the letters *CM* and a date. I don't remember what the date was, though. The only reason I remember the initials is because your aunt mentioned they were yours."

I leaned back on the sofa, trying to make sense of everything. When Miles's phone rang, I passed it to him without even looking at it.

He talked for a few minutes, then he hung up. "That was my boss. He's in town and he needs to talk to me, so we're going to have to postpone going shopping."

I nodded, relieved. It would give me time to figure out what was going on with my aunt.

"Are you sure you're okay?" he said.

I nodded, and he gathered his things. "I'll give you a call tomorrow. Maybe we can go then and pick out something."

I sat for hours thinking about my conversation with Miles, but none of it made sense. I was heading into the kitchen to get something to eat when the phone rang.

"Hey, Corky," Aunt Dani said.

"Hey," I said dryly.

"Why you sounding all sad?"

"I've just got a lot on my mind," I said.

"What's up?"

I thought about telling her about the picture I had seen

on Miles's phone and what he had told me, but I couldn't figure out how to do it without accusing her of stealing. "Nothing. I'm fine, really," I said.

"Miles and I are about to go to Griffith Park, so while I was waiting on him, I thought I'd check on you."

"Really?" I said. "You talked to Miles today?"

"Yeah. I just got off the phone with him. Why?"

I didn't know what to say as I sat staring at Miles's cell phone, which he had left on our dining room table. "You called him on his cell?"

"Yeah. Why?"

I was getting more and more confused. Miles's phone hadn't rung since he had gotten the call from his boss hours earlier.

"Uh, Aunt Dani, I've got to go."

I hung up and was still staring at his phone when the doorbell rang. I opened it without even bothering to see who it was.

"Did I leave my phone?" Miles asked.

I pointed toward the table and he walked over to pick it up. He was on his way out when he finally looked at me. "You feeling better?" he asked. "You look kind of funny."

"Yeah. So what time are you meeting Aunt Dani at Griffith Park?"

He looked at me in confusion. "I'm not meeting your aunt."

"So you haven't talked to her today?" I asked.

He held up the phone. "How could I when I didn't have this?"

"You guys still here?" Momma asked as she and Cory walked through the door.

"I had to meet with my boss," Miles said. "We can go now if you'd like."

"That's okay," I said. "I have something to do."

Miles looked at me strangely. "Have you talked to Loretta?" he asked.

I opened my mouth, wanting with everything in me to lie, but instead I found myself saying, "Yes."

"What did she want?" he asked.

"She had to go before she could say." I rushed the words out, then looked at the ground. I felt Miles staring at me and glanced at him, then quickly looked at the ground again.

"Okay, well, if you talk to her again, tell her to call me," he said.

I just nodded. "See you later, Donna," he said to Momma.

"What was that all about?" Momma asked before he could get the door closed.

"I don't know," I said.

She shook her head. "I need to get ready for Bible study tomorrow night. I'll be in my room if you need me."

"Momma, can I go out for a while?" I asked.

She looked like she was about to say no. "I'll only be gone for a little while," I said. "I just need to go check on something real quick."

"Something like what?"

My mind raced as I tried to come up with a plausible excuse. "The Worth the Wait members and I want to do something for Andrea, and I promised them I would check into it. I just need to run to the mall."

"If you wait, I'll take you," she said.

"Momma, I can drive myself. What's the point of having my own car if you never let me drive?" I said. "Please."

She sighed. "Fine," she said. "Take your sister with you."

"Momma," I whined. Normally I didn't mind having Cory with me, but since I was going to track down my aunt, I didn't know what I would find.

"Either you take your sister or you don't go," she said.

I had stomped up two stairs before Momma called up to me. "Keep it up, and you won't be going anywhere."

I got to Cory's room, and she was lying across her bed, sleeping. I didn't even try and wake her. Instead, I ran back downstairs.

"She's asleep," I said.

Momma sighed. "Girl, get out of here before I change my mind."

"Thanks, Momma," I said, giving her a kiss.

"Be back here before it's dark," she said.

I glanced at my watch, realizing I had about two hours. "Yes, ma'am," I said.

"Do you have your cell phone?"

I checked my purse and realized it wasn't there, so I ran back up to my room and grabbed it. On the way back downstairs, I peeked in Cory's room and saw she wasn't on her bed anymore. I groaned, knowing Momma was going to make me take her.

I ran downstairs and was relieved when I didn't see her.

Figuring she was in the bathroom, I kissed Momma again and jumped in the car, and as much as I wanted to rev the engine and tear out the driveway, I didn't since I knew Momma was watching. I put on my seat belt, adjusted the mirrors, then waved at Momma, who waved back from the front window. I had barely made it around the corner before I was flying to Griffith Park where Aunt Dani had said she was going.

She was already there when I arrived, sitting on a swing. I parked at the far end of the lot and snuck back to her. My eyes widened in surprise when I saw Miles walking up.

Aunt Dani must have sensed his presence, because she looked up. "What are you doing here?" she asked.

"I could ask you the same thing," he said, looking angry.

"How'd you know I was here?"

"Your niece slipped up and told me," he said, and my eyes got big. I wondered if he knew I was there.

Aunt Dani looked around, and when she glanced in my direction, I ducked behind a bush so she wouldn't see me.

"Corky's here?"

Miles shrugged and looked around. "I don't think so." He looked in my direction, but I wasn't sure he saw me. I had never seen him look so hurt.

"What's going on, Loretta?"

"Baby, what are you talking about?" she said. She reached out to touch his arm and he turned to look at her.

"There's a bunch of stuff that isn't adding up with you," he said.

Aunt Dani looked at him curiously. "What are you talking about?"

"Are you seeing someone else?" he asked.

Aunt Dani laughed. "Why would you ask me something like that?" she said.

"Like I said, something's not adding up. In all the time I've known you, I've never been to your place. As far as I know, you don't work, yet you have all this expensive stuff, and I know it's not because I'm buying it for you."

Aunt Dani popped him on the arm. "Boy, stop being so paranoid. The reason I've never invited you to my house is because it's never clean. I didn't want you to know how horrible I was at housekeeping until after we got married." She looped her arm through his. "As far as the expensive stuff goes, I'm still getting money from some of the modeling gigs I did when I was in L.A." She sniffed like she was about to cry. "I can't believe you don't trust me."

Miles hugged her. "I'm sorry," he said.

They kissed, and I turned away, embarrassed I had witnessed their argument.

When Miles said, "I hadn't planned on doing this now...." I looked up.

Miles was down on one knee holding Aunt Dani's hand. "Loretta Danielle Dennis, since the moment I first laid eyes on you, I've known there is no other woman for me. Would you do me the honor of being my wife?"

Aunt Dani stood there, her mouth open in shock. When she didn't say anything, Miles stood and gathered her to him.

"I know I don't have a ring," he said. "I was going to

take Courtland to look at one today. We can go and pick out whatever you want.... Well, maybe I should say whatever I can afford." He gave a nervous laugh.

"Miles," Aunt Dani said, "I don't know what to say."

"Say yes," he said.

Aunt Dani nodded and Miles squeezed her tight and looked at her. "I have something to tell you," she whispered. Before he could respond she said, "I'm pregnant."

Miles's face lit up. My mouth dropped open and I started backing away. Aunt Dani was only twenty-one, and while I wasn't stupid enough to think she was a virgin, I thought she would at least have sense enough to protect herself.

I realized I had intruded enough and headed back to the car, tossing Cory's Game Boy into the backseat when I accidentally sat on it.

I couldn't believe Aunt Dani was pregnant, and she was getting married.

fourteen

I didn't feel like heading home, so I called Momma to ask if I could stay out a little longer. When she told me Andrea had called and wanted to talk to me, it was just the distraction I needed. I had been wanting to talk to her for a while anyway, and this was the perfect chance.

I had only been to her house once before when the members of Worth the Wait had had a sleepover.

"Hey, Courtland," she said, giving me a hug. I smiled afterward, knowing I would never forget the lesson I had learned the last time she hugged me. "It's good to see you."

"You, too," I said, making my way to her kitchen.

"You hungry?" she asked. "My boyfriend is coming over later, and I was just about to make some spaghetti."

"I didn't know you were seeing someone," I said.

She smiled. "His name is Justin Clarke. He's an associate minister over at Evergreen Baptist Church."

I nodded, really happy for her.

"I'm cooking dinner for him tonight. You want to help?"

"Sure." I went to wash my hands, then made my way over to the counter.

"Can you cut up those vegetables for the salad?" she asked.

I grabbed a knife and started slicing a cucumber while she added a whole head of garlic to a pot of spaghetti sauce. We normally used the jarred sauce, so I wasn't sure if she was supposed to add that much. I thought at most it should be one or two cloves, but since I wasn't sure, I didn't say anything.

"So you've had a lot going on lately," she finally said.

"Yeah, the last few months have been crazy," I said.

"How are you feeling about everything that's going on with Allen?"

"I was kind of hurt," I said honestly, "but I'm glad that the charges have been dropped."

"Do you think he raped that girl?"

"Yes," I said before I could stop myself.

She looked at me curiously. "What makes you so sure?"

Like a dam, everything that had happened between me and Allen came bursting forth, and Andrea listened in silence. When I was done, she looked at me. "That's a lot for one person to carry around," she said softly.

I felt drained after sharing the story with her, like all the energy had been zapped out of me. Bree was the only other person who knew everything, but Andrea was the only adult who knew.

"Why would he use me like that, Andrea?" I said as I angrily chopped a cucumber. "I thought he really cared for me. I was looking at condoms...." I glanced at her to see her reaction, but she was busy stirring the sauce. "He only bet ten dollars. Is that all I'm worth?"

Andrea stilled my hand, then pulled me into a hug. "You tell me. Is that all you're worth?"

"No," I said. "Why would you ask me that? Of course I'm worth more than that."

"It seems to me like you've let Allen be the one to determine your worth," she said. "From what I'm hearing, you've allowed him to say horrible things to you and get away with it. He keeps track of you wherever you go, he tells you what to wear, he wanted you to sleep with him even though you told him that's not what you wanted, he's put his hands on you several times and he tried to rape you."

"I know," I said. It sounded horrible when she said everything out loud.

She led me to the kitchen table, and we sat down. "Did you see any red flags from the beginning?" she asked.

I thought about a few things Allen had said and done that had really bothered me, but I had brushed them off as signs that he really loved me. "Yeah, I saw them," I admitted.

"Why didn't you listen to them?"

"Because I thought he was just doing them because he loved me."

"Maybe he was doing them because you didn't love you," she said.

"I love myself," I protested.

"Really?"

I thought about it. "I do," I said, but I wasn't so sure I believed it.

"If you loved yourself, you would never compromise your beliefs for anyone. Those little red flags are God's way of telling you something is wrong. You have to learn to listen to them. God is trying to teach you something, and he's going to keep repeating it until you listen. I don't want you to be somewhere clinging to life before you finally learn your lesson."

I thought about my conversation with Andrea all the way home. After dinner, I headed to my room, still thinking about Andrea and Aunt Dani. They weren't that far apart in age, but they were so different. After I had gotten over the shock of Andrea being HIV positive and Aunt Dani being pregnant, I had started thinking about my conversation with Miles earlier. I thought of the picture I had seen of Aunt Dani wearing my purity necklace, and I wondered how she'd gotten it.

I took a nap and was just headed downstairs to get a load of laundry out of the dryer when the phone rang, scaring me so bad I jumped. It wasn't that late, but Momma and Daddy had gone out on a date and they'd dropped Cory at her friend Destini's house, so the phone sounded louder in the empty house.

"Hello," I said as I heard my mother pick up the other extension. I didn't realize she was back home.

Someone said something, but they were on a cell phone and the call started breaking up.

"Hello," I said again.

The first part of the call was muffled, but I heard the word *Dani* before the call dropped.

I frowned in confusion and headed upstairs, but Momma was already walking toward me. "Who was that?" we asked at the same time.

I shrugged, then it occurred to me to look at the caller ID. The number didn't show up, so I tried *69 and got a busy signal. I was about to try again when the phone started ringing and Momma snatched it from me before I could answer.

"Hello," she said, then she stopped and listened. "I'm her sister." The blood drained from her face. "Are you sure? I'll be right there."

She hung up the phone and ran upstairs, and I ran after her. "What's wrong?" I asked.

Momma didn't say a word as she ran into the room and threw on some clothes. "Momma, what's wrong?"

"Dani's hurt," she said.

"What?" I said.

"She's been hurt. She's at the hospital. Go get your sister."

"Isn't she at Destini's house?" I asked.

"Oh, yeah," she said absently.

"I'm going with you," I said. Luckily, I was dressed ready to roll as Momma called it. I had on sweats and a T-shirt, so I just had to throw on some shoes.

"Call your daddy and your grandparents," Momma said as she focused on driving.

I reached for my phone and realized I didn't know how to get in touch with Daddy, since I hadn't called him in a long time. "What's his number?" I asked.

"What?" Momma said, sounding distracted as she took her eyes off the road for a brief second.

I glanced up just in time to see us veering into the other lane. "Momma," I yelled.

She looked at the road and jerked the steering wheel as the sound of a horn filled the car.

"Are you okay?" she asked.

I nodded, my heart beating so fast I thought she could hear it.

I decided to let Momma focus on the road. I grabbed her cell phone and scrolled through until I found Daddy's work number, then called him. The dispatcher patched me through and I briefly told him about Aunt Dani being in the hospital.

"I'll be right there," he said.

As he promised, he was waiting on us when we arrived at University Hospital.

"Corwin," Momma said, rushing to him.

He held her close and whispered in her ear, and she nodded as she tried to fight back tears. "Do you know what happened?"

Daddy shook his head. "One of my co-workers was patrolling Griffith Park when he found her in the parking lot. It looks like an attempted robbery. He found our number in Dani's purse and had someone call you. When someone from the office realized she was my sister-in-law, they called me," he said and took a deep breath. "It doesn't look too good. She was hurt pretty bad. She was barely breathing when they got to her."

Momma started crying, and Daddy rubbed her back. Cory and I just stood there in shock. I kept waiting for some sign that this was just a bad dream, like the one I had had on the first day of school when I dreamed I had fallen in front of Allen, only a thousand times worse. But when the doctor came out a few hours later, I knew it was real.

"Are you related to Loretta Dennis?" the doctor asked.

Momma nodded and sniffed. "I'm her sister," she said quietly. "Is she all right?"

"We don't know yet," the doctor said honestly. "She has head trauma, and both her arms are broken." He repeated a lot of what Daddy had said. "We'll know more over the next few hours."

"Can we see her?" Momma asked.

"Only for a few minutes," the doctor said. "She's heavily sedated, so she probably won't know you're there."

Daddy thanked the doctor, and Momma turned to head toward Aunt Dani's room.

"Momma, I want to go, too," I said. She held out her hand, and I grasped it, and together we walked down the hall.

I don't know what I was expecting, but what I saw made me start crying.

Aunt Dani was hooked up to a bunch of monitors, and

her face was so swollen I barely recognized her. Her hair was matted with what looked like blood. Both her arms were in casts, and there was a tube down her throat.

"Oh, Dani," Momma said and started praying.

I just stood there, wondering who could have done something like this, then the image of Aunt Dani and Miles at the park flashed in my head. The room started swimming, and I had to sit down.

I took a couple of deep breaths, then on shaky legs I walked out of the room and headed over to Daddy, who was talking to another guy in uniform.

I stood in a trance, not really listening to the conversation, trying to make myself believe Miles hadn't done this to my aunt. He had looked so happy when she told him about the baby.

"How's the baby?" I asked, without really thinking, and Daddy and the other officer looked at me.

"What did you say?" Daddy asked.

"Aunt Dani…" I took a deep breath. "How's her baby?"

Daddy frowned at me. "What are you talking about?"

"She was pregnant, right?" I asked.

Daddy shook his head slowly. "No."

It was my turn to frown. "Are you sure? I heard her tell someone she was pregnant."

Daddy opened his mouth, but the other officer stopped him.

"When did you hear this?" the officer asked.

I told the story of following Aunt Dani to the park and her conversation with Miles.

"Can you think of anything else?" the officer asked, and I shook my head.

"No."

He said a few words to Daddy, then he was gone.

"Is Miles going to jail?" I asked.

"It looks that way," Daddy said.

Miles was picked up and brought in for questioning. Part of me felt bad, but part of me hoped he would go to jail for what he had done to my aunt.

Cory stayed home from school with me the next day. Momma had spent the night at the hospital, and Daddy was helping look for evidence to make sure Miles stayed in jail a long time.

I was fixing lunch when the house phone rang.

"Hello," I said, trying to open a loaf of bread while I held the phone perched between my shoulder and ear.

"Hey, baby, how you doing? I heard about your aunt and Miles. That's messed up. How's she doing?"

I didn't want to be moved by hearing Allen's voice, but my heart skipped a beat without my permission. "We don't know yet," I said.

"How are you?"

"Scared," I said.

"I'm coming over," he said.

"My parents aren't here," I said lamely. After all that had happened, I felt stupid that part of me wanted to see him.

"I think they'll understand you need me right now. I'll see you in a few minutes."

Cory and I were just finishing our food when the doorbell rang. I got up to answer it, and when I saw Allen, I forgot about all that had gone on between us and just melted into him, finding comfort in his arms.

"It's okay," he said, rubbing my back the way I had seen Daddy do to Momma. "I'm here." He started kissing on me, and I didn't want to admit how good it felt.

"Let's go up to your room," he whispered.

I pushed away from him, not believing he could be thinking about sex at a time like this, but he gathered me close. "Come on, baby. No one's here."

I thought about how he had tried to rape me a few days ago, and I couldn't believe how I was about to fall for him again. What was I thinking even letting him come over?

I was just about to tell him to leave when I jumped at the sound of breaking glass. I turned and Cory was standing there staring at us as juice dripped down her arms.

"Munchkin," I said, rushing over to her, "are you okay?" I moved her out of the way and started picking up the big pieces of glass. I looked at my sister and realized she had spilled the juice all over herself. "Go change your clothes."

She headed upstairs without a word.

"What's up with your sister?" Allen asked.

I shrugged before I headed into the kitchen to get the dustpan and broom. "You need to leave," I said, not even bothering to look up at him.

"So do the cops know what happened to your aunt?" he asked, totally ignoring me.

"Did you hear what I just said? You need to leave."

"Baby, why are you acting this way?" he said, trying to wrap his arms around me.

I held the broom in front of me, using it as a shield. "Allen, I'm serious. You've got to go. I don't want to see you anymore."

He laughed. "Oh, we're back to this again," he said. "What did I do wrong this time?"

I looked at him like he was crazy. "You're tripping," I said. "Is it just me, or did you not almost rape me a few days ago?" I realized how loud I was talking and lowered my voice. "I don't want to see you again."

Allen laughed even harder. "Baby, I know you're new to this whole sex thing. I didn't try to rape you. I was just trying to motivate you. I knew you were scared." He gave this devilish grin and I resisted the urge to hit him with the dustpan.

"I would never hurt you, Courtland. I love you too much to hurt you." He placed a gentle kiss on my chin. "I'm sorry if I gave you the impression I was going to hurt you. I had been drinking that night. I know that's no excuse, but it had me acting crazy. Plus, you were teasing me looking all good.... Forgive me?"

He looked at me with puppy-dog eyes, and I felt myself caving in. Maybe I had overreacted. He must have seen me melting because he leaned toward me and pulled me close. His touch brought me back to reality. I might not have any sexual experience, but I wasn't stupid. Allen had tried to rape me and he had started dating me because of a bet to sleep with me. He tightened his grip on my arm, and it reminded me of the other times he had grabbed me.

"You know I would never hurt you, right?" he said, his voice sounding on the verge of anger.

My mind raced as I tried to figure out how to get out of this situation. Allen was in my house, and the only one there with me was Cory.

"Yeah, baby, I know," I said, trying to sound sexy. "My daddy will be home soon, and you know how my parents trip when someone is in the house."

I had never prayed so hard for my daddy to come home.

"He needs to get used to me being around," Allen said. "You're my woman, and I can see you anytime I want. Your daddy needs to understand that."

I gulped.

"Let's go upstairs," he said, grabbing my hand.

"I need to go check on my sister," I said, glancing at the door, hoping he would get the hint.

Daddy chose that moment to walk in, and I ran over to him. "Hey, Daddy," I said, giving him a kiss for the first time in years.

Daddy took in Allen, who had stood from the sofa. "How you doing, Mr. Murphy?" he asked, putting the dimple in his right cheek on display as he extended his hand.

Daddy rested his hand on his service gun. "Courtland isn't allowed to have company when no one's home," he said.

"I'm sorry, sir. I wasn't thinking. I heard about Courtland's aunt, and I rushed over here without calling first. It won't happen again."

I snorted under my breath at the lie. Allen had been doing all his big talk, implying my parents weren't in control, but all that changed when he saw my daddy's gun.

Allen turned to me. "I'll call you later, Courtland."

"Whatever," I said, the word slipping out before I could catch it.

Allen didn't respond as he made his way toward the door.

As soon as it slammed, Daddy turned toward me, and I got scared.

I was surprised when he held his arms out to me, beckoning me to come to him. I hesitated before rushing into his arms. It felt good to be there. I felt protected, like I did when I was little, when I still believed my daddy was the bravest man in the world.

"Are you okay?" he asked softly.

His words made me tremble. I didn't want to admit how scared I was about Allen's presence, but truthfully I was.

"Courtland, I'm so sorry," he said, stroking my hair.

"It's okay," I said, but I don't know why I was saying it.

He took a deep breath and pushed me away from him. "No, it's not okay. It's my job to protect people, and I haven't even been protecting the ones in my own home."

I looked at him in confusion.

"Has that boy been putting his hands on you? You looked scared to death when I walked through the door."

My eyes got wide, but I didn't say anything, scared of what Daddy would do.

Daddy nodded, then turned toward the door.

"Where are you going?" I asked, running after him.

"I'm going to kill him," Daddy said calmly, and I knew he wasn't playing.

"Daddy, don't," I screamed, grabbing his arm.

He turned to me, and there was murder in his eyes, but for some reason I wasn't scared of him. "He put his hands on you?"

I gave a small nod.

Daddy drew his lips into a thin line. "Did he do anything else?"

I had been holding everything in for so long, it felt good to finally release it. "He tried to rape me," I said.

Daddy left without another word.

I sat up all night, waiting to see news of Allen's death on TV, but it never came. It wasn't until I was flipping through the channels that I realized it was the day of the NBA draft announcement. I sat watching for hours to see Allen. When his picture came up, I leaned forward, waiting for them to show a live shot of Allen. Instead an anchor appeared.

"As if Allen Benson's recent legal troubles aren't enough, the player who was thought to be a first-round draft pick is being investigated for accepting money and gifts from at least two NBA coaches."

My mouth fell open. Allen's life just couldn't get any worse. Before I could stop myself I laughed. Actually, if my daddy caught him, his life would be a nightmare.

Momma was still at the hospital with Aunt Dani, and although she hadn't woken up, the doctors were hopeful she would any day. Cory and I had gone to see Aunt Dani earlier that day, and after we returned home, she was quiet, even for her.

I went to check on her in her room where she was playing her Nintendo Wii.

"Hey, munchkin," I said, standing next to her.

She didn't say anything as she focused on the game.

"You okay?" I asked. "You've been pretty quiet the last couple of days."

When she didn't speak, I grabbed one of the controls from her. "You hungry?" I asked, forcing her to look at me.

When she looked up, I saw her eyes were red from crying.

"What's the matter?" I asked.

"It's my fault," she said.

I gathered her to me. "What are you talking about?" I asked.

"Aunt Dani's going to die, and it's my fault."

I rocked her. "She's not gonna die," I said, praying I was right. "Besides, Miles is the one who hurt her."

Cory sat back and shook her head. "No, he didn't," she said.

I frowned. "Yes, he did. I saw him there with Aunt Dani."

She shook her head harder, her glasses slipping down her nose, then she started crying again.

"Miles didn't do it," she insisted.

I thought about protesting again, but my sister seemed so sure of what she was saying, I decided to listen.

"If Miles didn't do it, who did?" I asked.

"Allen," she said, and burst into tears.

I sat there stunned. "What?" I said weakly. "Munchkin, why would you say something like that?"

"It's true," she said.

"But how do you know?"

"I snuck into the backseat the day you went to the park to find Aunt Dani," she said.

I thought she was making it up until I remembered her Game Boy being on the seat and the other time she had snuck into the car when I had gone shopping with Aunt Dani.

"You left before I could get back to the car, so I was going to ask Aunt Dani for a ride," she said. "After Miles left, Allen came."

Her eyes got big again, and she started shivering.

"They were kissing and stuff, then Aunt Dani told Allen she was pregnant with his baby, and he got mad. They started fighting, then he hit her...."

I forced myself to talk. "What?"

Cory reached over to her nightstand table and pulled open the drawer.

"What are you doing with my phone?" I asked when she handed it to me.

"It's not yours," she said softly.

I tried to turn it on, but the battery had died, so I went and got my charger and plugged it in. When a screensaver came up of Aunt Dani and Allen kissing, my mouth dropped open.

I started scrolling through the pictures she had saved,

and it seemed like there were hundreds of Aunt Dani and Allen together.

I couldn't believe my aunt had been seeing my man behind my back for what looked like the entire time I had been seeing him.

I sat there with tears streaming down my face.

Cory hit a button on the phone, and suddenly a video started playing. I watched as Allen hit my aunt a few times. When he tried to leave, she ran after him and hung on to the car door. I felt sick as I watched her fall down and Allen run over her. He got out of the car, looked at her, then got in the car and drove off without calling for help.

It took me a few seconds to comprehend that they were in Griffith Park where Aunt Dani had been the last time I had seen her.

"How did you get this?" I whispered.

"When they started fighting, Aunt Dani tried to call for help, but Allen grabbed her and started shaking her arm so hard the phone landed near me. I took it and started recording everything," she said.

I sat there still trying to take everything in. "How did you get home that night?" I asked.

"I caught the bus," she said.

"Girl, are you crazy? You can't just be running all over the city by yourself."

"Why not? You did that night you snuck out to see Allen." She said like it made all the sense in the world.

"Munchkin, I'm seventeen. You're just a kid," I said. I didn't even realize she knew about that night.

She looked hurt at my words.

"I just don't want you to get hurt," I said. "I wish you'd called me. I would have come to get you."

"I did call you," she said. "I was at the bus stop when I called. Someone let me use their phone."

I remembered the phone call we had gotten and how I had thought it was Allen.

"That was you?" I asked.

She nodded.

"You were supposed to be at Destini's house."

She shrugged and looked kind of sad. I felt horrible I had been so caught up in my own problems I hadn't even noticed my sister wasn't where she was supposed to be, and apparently neither had my parents.

We sat there in silence for a few minutes, and I grabbed the phone again and started going through the pictures. I realized a few of them must have been taken in Aunt Dani's apartment, since the background in a lot of them looked the same. She had on my Worth the Wait necklace in a few of the pictures as well as the earrings that had been stolen from the mall, and I recognized a few things that had been stolen from our house.

"We have to tell Daddy," I said.

Cory's eyes got big again and she shook her head. "Allen might get me," she said, sounding scared.

I gave her a hug, trying to reassure her. "I'm not going to let him put a hand on you," I said, really meaning it.

"If he hit you and Aunt Dani, he'll hit me, too," she said.

I tried to play dumb. "What are you talking about?"

"I heard you and Daddy talking last night. I know Allen hit you," she said. "I know everything."

I wanted to deny it, but I couldn't. I was tired of hiding from the truth. I realized I had to be honest with Cory so she would never find herself making excuses for a guy who was putting his hands on her—or worse.

"We need to talk," I said.

Cory and I stayed up late that night, and I told her about my relationship with Allen, how I had seen red flags when he had said and did things that made me feel uncomfortable, but I had ignored them because I really liked him.

I told her about how I was going to rededicate myself to Worth the Wait because I had come to learn how important my virginity was, and that being a virgin wasn't something people should be ashamed of. I also decided I was going to step down from my position as co-captain of the cheerleading squad. Being a cheerleader had never been my dream, and I was tired of doing what other people thought I should. I was going to follow my dream and try out for the girls' basketball team.

When Cory finally dozed off, I lay beside her, realizing I had to set an example, not just for her, but other girls out there, and that wasn't going to happen if I kept silent.

I must have dozed off, because when I woke up, Momma and Daddy were standing over me.

"How's Aunt Dani?" I asked.

"She flatlined...." Momma said, tears filling her eyes.

I had seen enough episodes of *House* and *ER* to know

that's what happened when someone died. Tears welled up in my eyes.

"The doctors were able to revive her, and they think she's going to be okay," Daddy said.

I breathed a sigh of relief.

"What happened to Allen?" I asked, looking at Daddy, expecting him to say he was dead.

"I just got word the cops picked him up at the airport. Apparently he was trying to head to New York."

"How did they find him?" I asked.

"I had an APB out for him," Daddy said. "I'm heading to the precinct now. I need to have a little talk with him."

I watched as his face changed, and I figured he was thinking about what Allen had done to me. "There are some other things you'll probably need to talk to him about," I said. I ran upstairs and grabbed Aunt Dani's cell phone, pushed the button so the video would play, then handed it to them. Momma's face went pale as she watched in silence and the muscle in Daddy's jaw twitched.

After they finished watching it, I showed them the pictures of Aunt Dani. Daddy scrolled through them and stopped at one of Aunt Dani hugged up with some guy.

"That's Luscious," he said, tapping the screen.

"Who?" Momma and I asked.

"The guy who was killed in the house."

"Aunt Dani knew him?" I whispered.

"Oh, Dani," Momma said. "What have you done?"

Daddy started scrolling through Aunt Dani's text messages, which I hadn't thought to do, and shook his head.

"What?" I asked, peeking over his shoulder.

I read a couple of the messages, and I realized how tight things had been for Aunt Dani since she left L.A. Apparently when Triple T had broken up with her, he had left her broke. She had been pretending she had all this money, but that wasn't the case, and it looked like she had started stealing to hide the fact that she was dead broke.

"She stole from her own family because she didn't want us to know she was broke?" I asked, shaking my head.

"She could have stayed with us," Momma said.

"If she needed someone to take care of her, why didn't she just marry Miles?" I said. "He really loves her."

"He probably didn't make enough money. Allen was about to make millions once he signed with the NBA," Daddy said.

"But he was my boyfriend," I said, suddenly getting angry at my aunt and Allen.

Momma gave me a hug. "I'm sorry you had to go through all this," she said.

I didn't have any words.

"I'm going to head over to the precinct," Daddy said, breaking the silence. He had just walked out of Cory's room when he turned around. "How did you get this phone?"

I thought about protecting my sister, but I realized I had hidden enough from my parents to last a lifetime. "Cory gave it to me," I said quietly. We glanced at my little sister, who had managed to sleep through our conversation.

Daddy sighed. "I'll try to keep her from having to testify, but I don't know if I'll be able to."

"If it will help any, I'll go down to the precinct and make a statement," I said, then I thought about Allen almost raping me and his physical abuse. "I want to press charges against him, too."

Momma and Daddy looked at me in surprise, and I knew Daddy had told Momma everything. "I've let Allen get away with enough. I'm not going to let him get away with what he did to me," I said. I took a deep breath, preparing myself for the fight that was to come.

Later that morning we headed to the police station, where Cory and I both gave statements. By the time we were done, it was midafternoon.

I walked over to Momma, who was sitting half-asleep at Daddy's desk.

Momma gently rubbed my face. "I'm proud of you, baby," she said. "I know that wasn't easy."

"I thought he loved me," I said, suddenly feeling sorry for myself. All I had wanted was a boyfriend, someone who would love me. "What's wrong with me that he couldn't love me?"

"Sweetie, there's nothing wrong with you. You weren't the problem. Allen was."

I thought about what she had said, and I realized she was right. I had been the best girlfriend I knew how to be to Allen, even compromising some things I had vowed I never would, but that hadn't stopped Allen from believing he had a right to put his hands on me.

Momma patted my cheek. As she was moving her hand, a sparkle caught my eye.

"What's this?" I asked, holding up her hand to look at the engagement ring. It was gold, and the diamond looked like it was at least a carat.

Momma laughed shyly. "Your daddy proposed. We're getting married," she said.

I looked up in surprise.

"Yeah, your mother's finally going to make an honest man out of me," Daddy joked, catching the tail end of our conversation.

I threw my arms around them and Cory, realizing I wouldn't change a minute of the last few months. Although I wouldn't wish what had happened on my worst enemy, it had made me stronger, and I was a better person because of having known and loved Allen Benson.

I vowed I wouldn't be a fool and make the same mistakes twice.

I walked out of the police station and headed to the Waffle House with my family. We sat crammed into a tiny booth, laughing and talking as we made plans for the wedding Momma had always dreamed about. Momma was taking her first step toward learning to love herself, and so was I.

* * * * *

A READING GROUP GUIDE

THE PLEDGE

The questions and discussion topics that follow are intended to enhance your group's reading of THE PLEDGE by Chandra Sparks Taylor. We hope this novel provided an enjoyable read for all your members.

QUESTIONS FOR DISCUSSION

1. Courtland received a lot of red flags in her relationship with Allen, but she chose to ignore them. What are some red flags that you've ignored in your relationships?

2. After meeting Allen, Courtland often questioned the pledge she had taken to remain a virgin until she got married. What beliefs have you compromised because of a relationship?

3. Bree proved to be a great friend. What are some signs a person is being a good friend to you?

4. Courtland was not always a good friend to Bree. Do you consider yourself a good friend? What ways do you show it?

5. Courtland was often bothered by her relationship with her father. Describe your relationship with your parents or guardian. Name some ways you can make the relationship better.

6. Courtland's parents, especially her mother, were strict. Pinpoint some ways they were too strict, as well as ways they weren't strict enough. Do you believe her parents were justified in their behavior? Why or why not?

7. Aunt Dani gave Courtland a lot of bad advice and eventually hurt Courtland. What is some of the bad advice Aunt Dani gave? What is some bad advice you've been given?

8. Andrea served as a good adult role model for Courtland. How did she do so? What is some good advice she gave?

9. Was Courtland a good role model for her little sister, Cory? Why or why not? Do you believe you are a good role model? Why or why not?

10. Courtland and her mother both came to the realization they needed to learn to love themselves. What are ways they showed this? What are ways you can show you love yourself?

11. Courtland often felt pressure to continue her relationship with Allen. Discuss a time you've felt pressured to do something you didn't really want to.

12. Courtland's entire family was taken in by Allen's charm. Share a time when a person's behavior had everyone you know fooled.